The Never Girls

a dandelion wish

*

from the mist

written by
Kiki Thorpe

illustrated by
Jana Christy

A STEPPING STONE BOOK™
RANDOM HOUSE 🏠 NEW YORK

For Roxie

—*K.T.*

For Johnny

—*J.C.*

randomhousekids.com/disney
ISBN 978-0-7364-3460-7
Printed in the United States of America
10 9 8 7 6 5 4 3 2 1

Never Land

Far away from the world we know, on the distant seas of dreams, lies an island called Never Land. It is a place full of magic, where mermaids sing, fairies play, and children never grow up. Adventures happen every day, and anything is possible.

There are two ways to reach Never Land. One is to find the island yourself. The other is for it to find you. Finding Never Land on your own takes a lot of luck and a pinch of fairy dust. Even then, you will only find the island if it wants to be found.

Every once in a while, Never Land drifts close to our world . . . so close a fairy's laugh slips through. And every once in an even longer while, Never Land opens its doors to a special few. Believing in magic and fairies from the bottom of your heart can make the extraordinary happen. If you suddenly hear tiny bells or feel a sea breeze where there is no sea, pay careful attention. Never Land may be close by. You could find yourself there in the blink of an eye.

One day, four special girls came to Never Land in just this way. This is their story.

Never Land

Pirate Cove

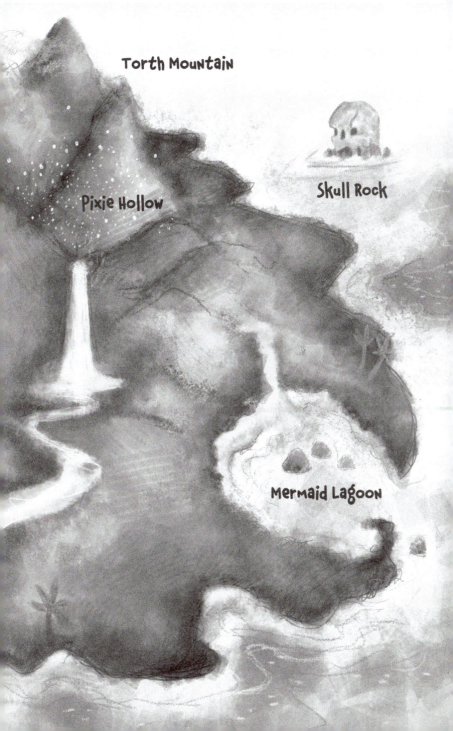

Torth Mountain

Pixie Hollow

Skull Rock

Mermaid Lagoon

It seemed to Kate as if they
were swimming through the air.
She felt a thrill travel
from the tips of her toes to the
top of her head.

Disney
The Never Girls

from the mist

written by
Kiki Thorpe

Illustrated by
Jana Christy

A STEPPING STONE BOOK™
RANDOM HOUSE 🏠 NEW YORK

chapter 1

Kate McCrady opened one eye, then the other. Early-morning sunlight streamed across her face.

Kate blinked, still half asleep. Was she in her own bedroom at home? Was she sleeping under the weeping willow tree in Never Land? For a moment, she didn't know. She pushed her tangle of red hair out of the way and saw a large dollhouse in the corner.

Oh, that's right, Kate thought. She was at her best friend Mia Vasquez's house, sleeping over. Lainey Winters was there, too, bundled in a sleeping bag a few feet away.

Kate tried to send them a silent message: *Wake up! Wake up, so we can go back!*

Only a few days before, Kate, Mia, Lainey, and Mia's little sister, Gabby, had found a secret portal to Pixie Hollow, the realm of the fairies on the island of Never Land. Or rather, the portal had found them—even though the path to Never Land wasn't always in the same place, it always seemed to be where the girls could find it.

Kate loved their visits to Never Land. There she had no homework, no chores— nothing to do but explore. Adventure waited around every tree, hill, and bend along Havendish Stream. Kate couldn't wait to go back.

But her silent message didn't work. Lainey let out a gentle snore. Mia turned over, burrowing deeper under her covers.

Maybe a nudge would wake them. Kate stretched so her foot grazed the bottom of Lainey's sleeping bag. She scooted closer, then stretched again. This time, she bumped Lainey's leg.

Lainey sat up, blinking sleepily.

"I was just stretching," said Kate, trying to look innocent. "I didn't wake you, did I?"

"No . . . yes." Lainey fumbled around by her pillow. When she found her glasses, she put them on, a little crookedly. "Is Mia awake?"

"I am now!" cried Mia, pulling the pillow over her head. Kate could only see a bit of her long, dark curly hair poking out. "What time is it? It feels too early to be awake."

"It *is* early." Kate jumped up, leaped over Lainey, and bounced on Mia's bed. "Early enough to get back to Never Land."

Mia glanced at the clock. It said 6:30. "My parents won't be awake until at least seven."

"Exactly," said Kate. "And that could mean hours and hours in Never Land." The girls had discovered that time worked differently on their trips to Pixie Hollow. Hours could pass there, while at home

hardly a minute would go by. "Let's go now!"

Mia bolted upright as a thought came to her. "I hope Gabby kept our promise. I hope she didn't try to go to Never Land while we were sleeping."

On their last visit, the portal had closed, and Gabby had been stuck alone in Never Land. After that, the girls had made a promise to always go to Never Land *together*. But Mia was worried that Gabby wouldn't be able to resist going on her own anyway, since the portal was now in her room.

The three girls dressed quickly. Kate pulled her thick red hair away from her face with a barrette without bothering to comb it. Then she, Mia, and Lainey tiptoed across the hall to Gabby's room.

Inside the door, Kate stopped short. "Do you guys see what I see?" she whispered.

Lainey and Mia nodded. A dense mist hung over half the room.

Meanwhile, Gabby slept peacefully on her back, unaware of anything unusual. Her arms were spread wide, as if she were waiting for a hug.

"She looks so sweet," Mia said softly. "Maybe we shouldn't wake her."

Suddenly, Gabby sat up. "What's going on?" she said, looking around. "Why is my room so foggy?"

"I don't know. Something strange is happening," said Mia. "Look at the closet door."

A heavy mist hovered around the doorframe. More fog seemed to seep from

beneath the door—the door that led to
Never Land.

Kate rushed over. "I'll check it out."

"Wait, Kate. We all go together, or we
don't go at all," Mia reminded her.

Kate stopped with her hand on the
doorknob. "Hurry and get dressed, Gabby."

Gabby hopped out of bed. She slipped
a pink tutu and a pair of costume fairy

wings over her pajamas. "Ready!" she announced.

Kate pulled open the door. Gabby, Mia, and Lainey crowded behind her.

Inside the closet, fog swirled from floor to ceiling. It covered Gabby's toys and clothes. Holding hands, the girls stepped through the mist.

Kate heard a tinkling sound, like bells ringing. She took another step. Faint voices floated toward them.

"I hear the fairies!" Lainey said.

The voices grew louder as the girls crept forward. The walls around them curved, becoming the inside of a hollowed-out tree trunk.

Finally, they stepped out from the tree. They were standing on a grassy bank in Pixie Hollow. At least, Kate *thought* it was Pixie Hollow. It was hard to tell. Fog covered everything.

"I can barely see!" exclaimed Lainey. She wiped her glasses.

Kate shuffled forward a bit, squinting. "There has never been fog in Pixie Hollow before. It's always sunny when we visit."

She didn't see Havendish Stream until she almost walked into it. Now she could see the fairies whose voices they'd heard. They were water fairies paddling birch-bark canoes. The fairies called out to one another so their boats wouldn't bump.

"Watch out!"

"Where did this fog come from?"

"Go to the right, Silvermist!"

Spring, a messenger, flew over the

water, shouting to the fairies. "Everyone to the courtyard! Queen Clarion has called a special meeting!

"Oh!" She stopped inches in front of Kate. "I didn't know you girls were here. Better come, too!"

At the courtyard, Kate stared up at the Home Tree. The giant maple, filled with fairy bedrooms and workshops, usually sparkled with fairy glow. But today its branches were hidden in mist.

Around the girls, fairies crowded into the pebbled courtyard. They landed on the low tree branches, where they sat lined up like birds on a telephone wire. They chattered nervously, filling the air with a low hum.

"What's going on?" Kate asked a baking fairy, Dulcie, who was hovering nearby.

"Queen Clarion is worried about this fog. We all are. It is awfully strange weather for Never Land."

"What's causing it?" Kate asked.

Dulcie shrugged. "All I know is it's making the fairies hungry. At breakfast today, everyone ate like it was the Harvest Feast."

"Breakfast?" Kate's stomach rumbled. They hadn't had a chance to eat.

Dulcie winked knowingly. "I'll get you girls some treats right away!" Nothing made Dulcie happier than filling empty stomachs.

Moments later, serving-talent fairies delivered basket after basket filled with blueberry puffs. Each puff was the size of a marble. Kate ate two dozen.

Rain, a weather-talent fairy, flew by

carrying a medicine dropper. She pressed the dropper's bulb to draw in some mist. Then she peered at the droplets inside.

"Sure, it's a mist easter with foggish low bursts," she announced. Then she frowned. "But squalls are down."

"Is that good or bad?" Kate asked. But she was talking to herself. Rain had already flown away.

chapter 2

Mist in the morning, fairies take warning.

Silvermist stood in the courtyard, waiting with the other fairies for Queen Clarion to speak. But her thoughts strayed.

Mist in the morning, fairies take warning. Why couldn't she get that old fairy saying out of her head?

Silvermist tucked her long hair behind her ears. All morning, she'd felt uneasy. She'd been boating on Havendish Stream when the fog came. Silvermist had never seen such a heavy mist before. It had taken all her water knowledge to get her boat to shore without running into anything.

As a water-talent fairy, Silvermist liked water in any form—from dewdrop to rushing waterfall. Usually, just being near it soothed her. But this clammy mist made Silvermist shiver from wing to wing.

Why is it bothering me? she wondered. After all, mist was water, too.

As she thought about it, Silvermist noticed the four Clumsies kneel down behind her. *Girls. Not Clumsies,* she reminded herself. *They don't like to be called that.* She nodded hello to Kate, Mia, Lainey, and Gabby.

"Hi, Silvermist," the tall one, Kate,

said. "What do you think about this fog? You're a water fairy, so you must know what's going on."

Silvermist shook her head. "I'm afraid I don't."

"Well, that's helpful," said Vidia, a fast-flying fairy, as she swept past. "A water talent who doesn't have a clue about the water right in front of her nose."

Silvermist didn't bother to reply. Vidia always had something nasty to say. Still, the remark bothered her. Why *didn't* she know more?

Mist in the morning, fairies take warning.

"Fairies, sparrow men, and guests!" Queen Clarion finally spoke, interrupting

Silvermist's thoughts. "Gather close, so we can see each other more clearly."

Everyone edged forward.

"We don't know how long the fog will last," the queen said. "But it's too dangerous to fly in weather like this. There could be accidents. So for now, all fairies are grounded."

A murmur rippled through the crowd.

"What?" Vidia's voice rose above the others. "You can't mean fast-flying fairies, too? Why should we be punished?"

"No one is being punished, Vidia," the queen replied. "It's for your own safety."

"Couldn't there be exceptions?" Vidia asked, her voice sugary.

Out of the corner of her eye, Silvermist noticed Kate eagerly move closer, to see if she was "grounded," too.

Queen Clarion thought for a moment. "You're right, Vidia. There should be a few exceptions."

Vidia gazed around at the other fairies, a superior smile on her face.

"We'll need some fairies to stay on lookout, to make sure everyone is safe," Queen Clarion continued. "The scouts—and only the scouts—may fly."

Hearing this, the fairies grumbled, especially Vidia, who scurried away using her wings to help her walk faster.

After the meeting, fairies milled around in the courtyard. They seemed nervous about going anywhere on foot.

Fawn, an animal-talent fairy, came toward Silvermist. "Have you seen Beck, or any of the other animal talents?" she asked. "We need to bring in the dairy mice, but it could take ages walking. We'll have to work together to herd them."

"Can I help?" asked a voice behind Silvermist.

"Oh, Lainey, that would be wonderful," Fawn said. "You can cover much more ground than we can. And you can practice your mouse calls."

Lainey beamed, happy to be of use. She turned to Kate. "Do you want to come?"

Kate shrugged. "I don't speak Mouse. I'll find something else to do."

"Come with us!" Hem, a sewing-talent fairy, called from down by Kate's feet.

"Yes!" echoed Mia, taking Gabby's hand. "We're going to make some new doll clothes. Hem is going to help us."

Kate shook her head. "I'm not really

in the mood for sewing . . . ," she began, when a loud rumble rolled through the sky.

All the fairies stopped what they were doing and looked up. But there was nothing to see but fog.

"What was that?" Silvermist asked.

The rumble grew louder.

Myka, one of the scout-talent fairies, took off into the soupy air. Right away, Silvermist lost sight of her.

"The fog is moving," said Myka. Her voice came down faintly through the mist. Thunder sounded again, drowning out the rest of her words. But they didn't need to hear her. The fairies could see for themselves that the fog was roiling, gathering into great big swirls.

A gust of wind kicked up. Trees swayed. The fairies clung to each other. "Is it a storm?" Dulcie cried. Storms were rare in Never Land.

Suddenly, a shrill whinny split the air.

"That sounded like it came from the meadow!" cried Fawn.

Everyone ran toward the meadow. The fairies on the ground scrambled over tree roots and darted around clumps of flowers. Several fairies caught rides with the girls, who could run much faster with their long legs. Silvermist joined a group of fairies riding on Kate's shoulder.

The scouts flew and arrived at the meadow first. The girls got there just afterward. They all stood at the edge of the woods. No one wanted to go closer.

A huge cloud was rolling across the grass. It churned like rushing flood waters. The thunder was deafening. The earth trembled.

Then, as quickly as it had come up, the noise died down. The cloud blew away. In its place stood a herd of silver-white beasts with wispy manes and tails that trailed into mist. One of them shook its head. Another flicked its tail. Droplets of rain flew off them.

"Horses!" Kate murmured, her eyes wide.

"Not just horses," whispered Silvermist. "Mist horses."

Chapter 3

Kate stood at the edge of the meadow, gazing at the horses. Her friends, the fairies, and everything else fell away as she stared.

The horses were huge, and yet they looked light as air. The ends of their long manes and tails seemed to disappear into the mist. Their eyes were a ghostly gray. To Kate, they looked as if they'd come straight out of the sky, as if the wind and rain had brought them to life. Even in a magical place like Never Land, the horses seemed otherworldly.

"Mist in the morning, fairies take warning," whispered a voice at Kate's ear. It was the water fairy Silvermist.

"There's some sort of legend about the mist horses," Silvermist went on, almost as if she was talking to herself. "I think they bring trouble."

Several fairies nearby turned to look at her. "Trouble," repeated a sparrow man, sounding worried. Others frowned.

What kind of trouble could these creatures bring? Kate wondered. They looked so beautiful and peaceful.

"You know, I'm probably confusing mist horses with sea horses," Silvermist said quickly. "I'm sure it's nothing."

The animal-talent fairy Fawn spoke up. "I'll talk to the horses. Find out where they're from and why they're here."

Fawn fluttered closer to one of the animals. She stopped so she could look it in the eye and swung her long ponytail like a mane. Then she let out a *hmph,* followed by a snort and a whinny.

Kate thought she sounded just like a horse.

But the mist creature ignored her. Fawn tried again. This time, the horse turned its back. Fawn tried another horse, but it also turned away.

Fawn sighed loudly. "They're not telling me any—"

Suddenly, one horse flicked its tail, striking Fawn.

"Oh!" Fawn spun through the air like a top out of control.

Silvermist and Tinker Bell raced to her. They each caught hold of one of Fawn's hands. They whirled along with her until, bit by bit, they slowed. At last, they were able to land on a rock.

"Fawn, are you okay?" Tinker Bell asked.

Fawn nodded, dazed. "I—I think so."

"It's time to leave the meadow," Queen Clarion said. "It's too dangerous here."

Kate's heart sank. Leave? Now, when the horses had only just arrived? But most of the fairies seemed perfectly happy to go.

On the way back, Dulcie was already talking about the light-as-mist meringues she wanted to bake. Other fairies planned a game of hide-and-seek. "It will be extra fun in the fog!" said a sparrow man. Fawn, still too dizzy to walk, was riding on Lainey's shoulder.

Kate fell into step beside Mia. "I don't see why we have to go," she complained.

"It's probably better. They do seem kind of dangerous," Mia said with a glance at Gabby.

Dangerous? Kate thought. "Exciting" was a better word. Of course, if you were a five-year-old—or a five-inch fairy—it was a different story. Then it made sense to stay clear of the horses. But everyone always said Kate was tall for her age. She wouldn't be in any danger.

"So now you can help us with the doll clothes," Mia went on cheerfully. "We can start by sorting the petals and silk threads."

Mia kept talking, but Kate stopped paying attention. She really didn't want to go back to the Home Tree and sew doll clothes. Or even play fairy hide-and-seek.

The fairies, able to squeeze into knot-holes or inside flower petals, always won.

Kate wanted to run and jump! She always chose soccer over quiet games during recess at school. After sitting at a desk for hours, she needed to move. That was how she felt now, too.

Those horses! Kate could tell they also loved to run and jump. They were so . . . so *alive*!

Kate stopped. "I'm going back for another look," she told Mia.

"What?" Mia said, startled.

"I'll just be a minute," Kate promised. "I'll meet you at the Home Tree."

Before Mia could say anything else, Kate turned and ran back to the meadow.

She stood at the edge of the trees, afraid to go any closer.

The horses were still there, almost hidden in the mist. One bright, silvery mare stood at the edge of the herd. As Kate watched, the mare suddenly kicked up her hooves. She moved away from the other horses, galloping around the meadow's edge.

As the horse neared Kate, she slowed to a trot.

She sees me! Kate realized.

The mare stopped a few feet away. For an instant, Kate held her gaze. *What would it feel like to touch a mist horse?* she wondered.

Kate inched closer. Then closer still. Slowly, hardly daring to breathe, she reached out her hand. She half expected it to go through the horse, as if she were made of air.

But the mare was solid. Kate stroked her neck lightly, feeling the velvet fur and the muscle underneath.

She feels like a real horse! Kate thought. Or at least what she imagined a real horse would feel like. Before now, Kate had never touched a horse. The closest she'd come was riding the carousel in City Park, near her home. But she very much wanted to ride this horse.

Kate glanced around to make sure no one was watching. If she tried to ride and then fell off, she'd be so embarrassed! Then, feeling brave and silly at the same time, she took hold of the horse's mane as gently as she could. The horse flicked her ears but didn't move.

But the mare was much taller than Kate had realized. She had no idea how to climb on!

Looking around, Kate spotted a thick tree branch a few feet above her. Maybe if she could climb the tree, she could lower herself onto the horse's back.

"Don't move," Kate whispered. She scrambled up the tree trunk, glad for the time she'd spent climbing trees in Never Land, on lookout with the scouts. Kate inched along the branch until she was more or less above the horse. The mare, nibbling at the meadow grass, didn't seem to notice.

Using all the strength in her arms,

Kate lowered herself from the tree branch. Now she was dangling in the air above the horse.

"Steady now," she murmured. But just then, the horse took a step forward.

"No!" Kate gasped. Afraid it was about to run away, she let go quickly, landing squarely on the mare's back.

The horse took off. On the verge of falling, Kate reached out and grabbed a handful of the horse's long mane. She bounced all over its back. Her teeth rattled together. She expected to hit the ground at any moment. But she didn't.

At last, Kate pulled herself more or less upright. She tightened her grip on the horse and squeezed with her knees to try to balance. The horse sped up. Kate let out a panicked squeal, but she stayed on.

"Hey!" she cried. "I'm riding!"

The faster the horse ran, the smoother her gait became. She left the meadow and headed over a hill that led to more forest.

It seemed to Kate as if they were swimming through the air. She felt a thrill travel from the tips of her toes to the top of her head. Were the horse's hooves even touching the earth? Kate couldn't tell.

"How do I steer?" she wondered aloud. Kate leaned slightly to one side, as she would to turn her bike. She tugged gently on the horse's mane. The horse began to turn.

"Yes!" Kate pumped a fist in victory. Then she grabbed quickly for the horse's mane again. She needed to hold on with two hands to keep from falling off.

At last, the horse slowed to a trot and then to a walk. They were nearing the meadow again. "Thank you for the ride. You can go back to your herd now," Kate said.

But as they came through the trees, Kate saw that the meadow was empty. The horses were gone! In the distance, she heard whinnies and the sounds of branches snapping.

At that moment, the scout Myka swooped down from a treetop. "What are you doing here?" she asked Kate. "And on a horse!"

Kate grinned. "I was just going for a ride," she said casually. "Did you see the herd from up there?" She pointed to the tree where Myka usually stood lookout.

Myka shook her head. "It's hard to see anything in this fog," she admitted. "I did catch a glimpse of something moving. It could have been the horses. If it *was* them, they're heading toward Vine Grove, north of here."

"Vine Grove," Kate repeated. Perhaps she could go there, too.

Myka frowned as if she knew what Kate was thinking. "It's outside Pixie Hollow."

"I'll bring this horse to her herd. Then I'll come back to the Home Tree." Kate figured that she could get to Vine Grove in no time on the horse. Then she could run back on foot before anyone missed her. "I'll be fast," she told Myka.

"I don't think that's a good idea," Myka said. "Wait here and—"

But Kate was already galloping away.

chapter 4

Silvermist hovered in front of a high shelf in the Home Tree library. She was trying to find a book about the mist horse legend.

She looked over the leaf-books on the Myths and Legends shelf. "Maybe it should be called *Mists* and Legends." Silvermist laughed at her own joke, then glanced around, afraid she might be bothering another fairy. But she was alone.

"So where might this old story be?" Silvermist said. She pulled a book from the shelf. It was titled *Hailstones in the Hollow and Other Odd Weather Fables.*

She flipped through the pages. When she saw the words "mist horse," she stopped and skimmed the page.

"Oh no!" Silvermist dropped the book with a thud. No wonder that warning had

been echoing in her head all morning. According to the legend, the fairies were in danger!

It's just a legend, Silvermist reminded herself. Picking up the book with shaking hands, she placed it back on the shelf. *It's a story, that's all.* But Silvermist had learned that superstitious old fables sometimes had a kernel of truth. If even a little bit of the legend was true, she had to warn the queen.

After leaving the library, Silvermist hurried to the Home Tree and rushed up to the queen's chambers. She knocked, but there was no answer. She knocked again. Nothing.

Growing impatient, Silvermist flung open the door.

"Oh cockleshells," she groaned. No one was there.

But through the open sea-glass window, she heard fairies talking. "I saw Kate at the meadow." Silvermist recognized Myka's voice. "She was riding a horse."

Silvermist darted back the way she'd come and went outside. Myka stood on a low branch, talking to Queen Clarion. Mia, Lainey, and Gabby were there, too.

"That can't be right," Mia was saying. "Kate's never ridden a horse in her life."

"Queen Clarion—" Silvermist began. But the queen held up a hand.

"Just a moment, Silvermist," she said. "Myka was telling us something important. Are you sure it was Kate, Myka?"

"Of course I am!" Myka said. "I spoke to her. And she *was* riding one of the mist horses. She was leaving Pixie Hollow."

"No!" Silvermist gasped. This time, everyone turned to look at her.

"I went to the library," she explained. "I found an old legend about the mist horses. . . ."

Silvermist paused and glanced at the girls. After all, the legend might not be true, and she didn't want to frighten them.

"Go on," the queen said.

"Well, I read that the horses enchant their riders, so they keep riding and riding," Silvermist said.

"You mean, they can't get off?" Mia asked.

Silvermist nodded. "The rider believes the horse is loyal and obedient. But it's a trick. It's the rider who obeys the horse, as if under a spell."

"What does that mean?" Gabby squeaked in alarm.

Mia exchanged a horrified look with Lainey. "It means Kate might be in trouble."

"We have to find her!" Lainey said.

"But what about the fog?" asked Myka. "Even the scouts can't see in it."

"We'll need someone who can find their way through it," Queen Clarion said. "Silvermist, you have my permission to fly to find Kate."

"Me? Oh!" Silvermist hadn't expected to lead the mission. She opened her mouth to explain that she didn't understand the fog any better than anyone else, then closed it. After all, Kate needed their help.

"We should leave now," she said to the girls. "The longer we wait, the harder it could be to find her. Who knows how far Kate can get on a horse. Myka, are you coming?"

Myka shook her head. "Some of the animal-talent fairies are missing. We think they got lost trying to find the dairy mice. The scouts are out looking for them."

Silvermist squared her shoulders. So she would have to lead them on her own.

"When I last saw Kate, she was headed toward Vine Grove," Myka said.

Silvermist turned to leave, but the queen stopped her, adding, "And for Never's sake, everyone, be careful."

chapter 5

"Come on, girl!" Kate urged the horse. Shapes loomed up from the mist, becoming trees and rocks that passed in a blur. Riding in the fog reminded Kate of riding a bicycle at night. She couldn't see things until they were almost on top of them. Still, the horse seemed to know where she was going. They managed not to hit anything.

As they rounded a small pond, the horse slowed. Kate reached down and patted the horse's neck. She felt like she'd been riding her whole life. And what a way to explore Never Land!

Kate looked around, trying to get her bearings. Were they close to Vine Grove? The island, cloaked in fog, seemed as mysterious as the mist horse. Kate had the feeling that anything could happen. That she could see anything. Go anywhere.

Why shouldn't *I* go *anywhere?* Kate thought. *I can explore a bit first and then bring the mare back to her herd. One little detour won't make a difference.*

Besides, Kate reasoned, there was really no need to go right back. The horse—*her* horse—seemed to be enjoying the ride as much as she was. The longer Kate rode, the more certain of it she felt.

The horse was a wild, free creature.

She made Kate feel wild and free, too.

"Let's go to the beach!" Kate cried. She turned the horse around sharply. The mare's hooves kicked up puffs of mist, like little clouds.

"Cloud," Kate said. "That's what I'll call you." The name seemed as light and free as the horse itself.

They cantered over a hill and through a grassy field. A sand dune appeared in the fog. Cloud sped up one side of the dune. Kate leaned low over the horse's neck as they raced down the other side, onto the beach.

The mist was heavier here. It rolled up to the beach with every wave.

They rode along the sand. When they came to the water's edge, Cloud whinnied

loudly and charged into the surf. Waves splashed Kate's legs. She laughed out loud.

But Cloud didn't stop. Just when Kate thought she'd go under with the next wave, Cloud whirled around, taking Kate back up the beach.

Still laughing, Kate slid off Cloud's back. She removed her shoes, emptying water from them. Her jeans were soaked, but she was too excited to feel cold.

"Is anyone there?" a fairy voice called. It sounded like Myka.

Kate groaned inwardly. Now she'd have to explain what she was doing here, when she was supposed to be looking for the herd in Vine Grove.

As she opened her mouth to call back, another voice rang out. It sounded very close by, just on the other side of Cloud.

"Okay, you found me," a voice drawled with fake sweetness. "Congratulations, Myka. You caught me flying. But why go through all the trouble of tracking me down? I'm not bothering anyone here. Can't a fast-flying fairy have a little fun?"

Vidia! Kate realized. Myka hadn't been talking to Kate. She was talking to Vidia. Cloud, who blended into the mist, must be shielding Kate from their view.

"No one's trying to get in your way, Vidia," Myka said. "I was scouting for lost fairies."

"Well, I'm not lost. I know exactly where I am."

Kate stood still. She hoped Vidia and

Myka wouldn't notice her. This time, Myka would insist she go back. Then Cloud raised her head and snorted.

"Are you coming down with the fairy flu, Vidia?" Myka asked. "It wouldn't be a surprise in this damp weather. You should go home and have a nice hot cup of dandelion tea."

"I didn't sneeze," Vidia snapped. "*You* did. Don't try to trick me."

"Trick you?" Myka repeated, confused. "I'm not trying to do anything but keep you safe."

"Tell you what," Vidia said, her voice

sugary again. "If you can catch me, I'll go back with you."

Kate heard the fast fluttering of wings, then Myka sighing.

Silence fell. Had Myka flown off, too? Kate waited a few moments longer, then decided she and Cloud were alone.

I'll leave now, too, Kate thought. She could take a shortcut, going around the pond the other way to get to Vine Grove. Then she'd go back to the Home Tree.

"Okay," Kate whispered into Cloud's ear. "Let's get you to the herd."

There was no tree nearby. But this time, as Kate took hold of Cloud's mane, she managed to pull herself up with only a bit of struggle. Kicking her legs, she belly-flopped onto Cloud's back, then wriggled around so she was upright.

"Is anyone else here?" Myka called. "Water fairies? Sparrow men?" She paused. "Kate?"

But Kate didn't hear her. She was on her way to Vine Grove.

*

On horseback, Kate neared a thick copse of trees. Long green vines twisted around trunks and looped from branches.

"That must be Vine Grove!" Kate said.

Kate rode into the trees, following the sounds. As they went deeper into the grove, the trees grew closer together. Creeping plants covered the ground. The path became hard to follow.

Kate ducked her head as vines brushed

her face. Between the fog and the leaves, she could barely see.

Ahead, vines tangled together like a thick green wall. Cloud strained through.

"Oh!" Kate struggled, pushing . . . pulling . . . batting at leaves and stems. But the vines caught her up like a net, holding her fast.

Cloud kept moving, and Kate, trapped in the vines, swung into the air.

"Cloud!" she called. The horse stopped a few feet away. She looked back at Kate and whinnied, as if to say, *What on earth are you doing?*

Suspended in midair, Kate struggled and flailed. But she couldn't free herself from the vines. She needed Cloud to pull her out.

She called again. "Cloud! Here, girl!"
This time, Cloud stepped closer.

Slowly, Kate worked one arm free. She
stretched but couldn't reach Cloud. "Just
a little bit closer," she coaxed. The horse
toed the ground but didn't move.

All Kate could do was throw her legs
forward and back and begin to swing.

With every swing, she got a little closer to the horse. At last she'd worked herself forward far enough that the fingertips of her free hand grazed Cloud's mane. One more swing, and Kate flung her arm around Cloud's neck.

"Go!" she shouted.

Cloud took off, pulling Kate along with her.

The vines around Kate snapped free of the trees. The force swung her out of the vine trap and over Cloud's head, as if she were jumping from a swing when it had reached its peak. She landed hard on the ground.

Kate stood up shakily. Her bangs fell into her eyes, and as she reached up to swipe them away, she realized she'd lost her barrette. She spent a few moments searching for it, but it was nowhere to be seen in the dense undergrowth.

Kate turned in a circle, trying to get her bearings. Ahead, the trees thinned out a little. She could see the shapes of large animals moving among them. The herd!

"Go on, girl," she said to Cloud. "Your friends are right over there!"

But Cloud didn't move.

Why doesn't she go to them? Kate thought. Something was wrong.

Kate made her way toward the herd. As she drew closer, she could see the animals more clearly. They weren't horses after all. They were deer.

She'd been following the wrong herd!

Where were the mist horses?

Kate looked to where the trees thinned out even more. *If I were a horse, I'd rather be out in the open than in a dense forest,* she thought.

"Let's keep going," Kate told Cloud. They'd find the herd. It wouldn't be fair to Cloud to give up.

And besides, Kate was having too much fun.

Chapter 6

Back in Pixie Hollow, Silvermist and
the girls set out toward Vine Grove.
Silvermist flew in front. The girls walked
single file behind her, following a narrow
path. The path was faint and overgrown,
more a deer trail than anything. But it
was the quickest way to Vine Grove that
Silvermist knew.

Vine Grove was to the north of Pixie
Hollow. The trail went through the

woods and around a small pond. When Silvermist came to the edge of the pond, she stopped.

There in the mud were two crescent-shaped marks. *Hoofprints!* Silvermist realized.

"What is it?" asked Mia, coming up behind her.

"There," Silvermist said, pointing. "They're from a horse's hooves, I'm sure of it."

"If the herd came this way, there'd be more tracks. So it must be from the horse Kate is riding!" Lainey said. "Let's follow them."

"The thing is, they're headed south, toward the ocean," Silvermist said. "*Away from Vine Grove.*"

Mia frowned. "Myka said Kate was headed *toward* Vine Grove. We should go there."

"But this is a clue!" Lainey countered. "Don't you think we should follow it?"

Both girls looked at Silvermist. She realized they were waiting for her to decide what to do.

Silvermist looked down at the tracks, thinking. The hoofprints did seem like a good sign. On the other hand, Kate had told Myka that she was going to Vine Grove. Which way was right?

Silvermist took a deep breath and closed her eyes. *Trust your instincts,* she advised herself. *If I were on a mist horse, where would I go?* Behind her lids, Silvermist saw waves crashing. She felt the tug of the ocean.

Silvermist opened her eyes. "We should go to the beach," she said.

With Silvermist once again in the lead, the group set off. Before long, the woods gave way to marsh. They climbed over a dune, slipping and sliding down the soft sand on the other side. Fog still hid everything around them. But they could hear waves breaking and seagulls squawking, and Silvermist knew they'd reached the beach.

"Stay close," she instructed. "We don't want to get separated in the fog."

"Kate?" Mia shouted. "Are you here?"

"Kate! Kate!" Lainey and Gabby joined in. They walked up and down the water's edge, calling and searching. But there was no sign of Kate.

"She's not here," Gabby said finally.

"Maybe we should have gone to Vine Grove after all," Lainey said, glancing at Silvermist.

Silvermist nodded, feeling a knot in her stomach. She'd been so sure that this way was right. But maybe it was only her feeling for water that had drawn her toward the ocean. Maybe her instincts had let her down.

And now they had lost so much time!

"We'd better hurry," she said, "or we may never catch up with Kate."

The girls and Silvermist retraced their steps away from the beach. This time, Silvermist didn't stop to check for prints. She didn't want to waste another second.

Soon enough, they came to a thick wooded area. Long vines hung from the trees, twisting around trunks and plants.

"This must be Vine Grove!" Mia said, racing toward the trees. "Kate! Where are you?" she cried.

But once again, no one answered her.

The girls walked among the vines, looking all around. Silvermist flew close to the ground. She scoured the undergrowth for some sign that Kate had been there. But she saw nothing.

"I don't understand," Mia said. "If Kate's not here, where is she?"

Silvermist swallowed hard. "There's something I haven't told you. About the legend—"

She was interrupted by a shout. "Over here!" Lainey cried. "I found something."

They followed Lainey's voice through a tangle of vines. Lainey stood on the other side. She pointed to the ground. "These vines were trampled."

"Something big must have done this," Mia said, examining the vines. "Maybe a horse. What do you think, Silvermist?"

Silvermist nodded. "It's possible."

A short distance away, they found another tangle of broken vines. Between the leaves, something gleamed.

"Look!" Gabby cried, bending over to pick it up. "A barrette."

"It's *Kate's* barrette," Mia said. "So she *was* here!"

Silvermist blushed, her glow turning orange with embarrassment. She was sure she'd flown right past this spot before. How could she have missed something as obvious as a Clumsy's barrette? She was starting to wonder if she should be leading the girls at all.

"Silvermist," Gabby said, "what should we do now?"

Silvermist hesitated. She couldn't trust her instincts. They had led her astray once already. She needed a real clue.

A movement among the trees made Silvermist's heart skip a beat. She turned toward it, hoping to see Kate. But it was only a deer. The deer gazed silently at them for a moment. Then it turned and bounded away, shaking droplets from the wet leaves around it.

"I wish I could speak Deer," Lainey said. "I could have asked if it had seen Kate."

"Hmm," said Silvermist, not really listening. The deer had given her an idea.

She began to fly slowly over the ground, looking closely at the leaves and blades of grass.

"What are you doing?" Mia asked.

"The leaves and grass are covered with droplets of water from the mist," Silvermist explained. "So if something as big as a horse passed through here, it would shake the water off . . . like this!" Silvermist pointed to a path through the damp grass.

The girls squinted. "I don't really see anything," Lainey said.

But Silvermist could see it clearly. Each blade of grass was wet on one side and dry on the other. "A large creature has come this way."

"Are you sure it was Kate and the horse?" Mia asked. "And not a deer or something?"

"I'm not sure it was Kate," Silvermist

admitted. "But it was bigger than a deer. And right now, I'm afraid that it's our only clue. We have to keep going."

Before it's too late, she added to herself.

chapter 7

Cloud galloped down a hill covered with sweet-smelling primroses. Kate could just see the yellow blossoms peeking out from the drifting mist.

Kate giggled with delight and flung one arm into the air, as if she were riding a roller coaster. This time she wasn't afraid of falling off. "Yeehaw!" she yelled.

The ground leveled, and they trotted past a noisy waterfall. The rushing water gurgled and hissed, dropping from a rocky ledge into a deep blue pool.

A butterfly fluttered in front of them. Its bright blue color was startling in the sea of white mist. Kate sneezed, and the butterfly spiraled away in the whoosh of air.

Never Land was even more amazing than Kate had imagined—animals, flowers, fog, and all. She spurred Cloud on, eager to see more.

But wait, she reminded herself. *We have to search for Cloud's herd.*

And then what?

Kate had never cared much about having a pet, unlike Mia, who loved her cat, Bingo, and Lainey, who loved all animals. But now that she and Cloud

were together, Kate wanted a horse. She wanted *this* horse. If she and Cloud could stay together, Kate would have days like this all the time.

Oh, if only there was some way I could keep her! Kate thought.

"Caught you, Clumsy," a voice purred in her ear.

Kate jumped. She twisted around and saw Vidia flying next to her.

"Look who's taking in the sights of Never Land," Vidia said. "Seems we're both far from home. Lost, are you?"

"Of course not," Kate snapped. Truthfully, she wasn't sure how far away from Pixie Hollow she was. But she felt certain that when it was time to return, she could find her way. "I'm bringing this horse to its herd."

"I don't care much what you do," Vidia said. "But I'm heading back to Pixie Hollow. The fog seems to be getting worse in this direction."

Kate frowned. She didn't want any advice—especially not from Vidia.

"I'm not afraid of a little fog," she said. "Why should I be, when I have Cloud?"

"You really think you've trained a wild horse?" Vidia snickered.

Kate grinned. "Watch this! Go, Cloud!"

At that, Cloud took off, leaving Vidia far behind.

This time, they rode until Kate's arms and legs ached. Her belly grumbled with hunger. She hadn't had anything to eat except Dulcie's blueberry puffs, hours earlier. She thought Cloud must be worn out, too. But strangely, the horse never seemed to get tired.

When Kate spied an apple tree rising out of the mist, she stopped and hopped off the horse. She twisted two apples from the tree and held one out for Cloud.

The horse sniffed the apple but didn't take it.

"I thought horses were supposed to like apples," Kate said. "Oh well, more for me." She bit into an apple, crunching loudly. "My legs are tired." Kate looked around for somewhere to sit.

A short distance away, she spied a big black rock. "Let's rest over there," she said.

Kate peered at the rock. Had it just moved?

The rock stretched, growing larger.

Kate froze, stifling a cry. That was no rock. It was a bear!

The bear rose to its feet. Kate hoped it hadn't noticed them in the mist. If they could hide somewhere, maybe they'd be safe. Kate glanced around. The only thing she saw was the apple tree.

The bear started to lumber toward them. Kate dropped the apples she was holding and inched herself behind the tree. She stood as still as a statue, afraid to run and draw the bear's attention. Maybe, by some miracle, it would pass them by.

The bear advanced until it was so close she could hear it grunting. She could see the droplets of mist on its thick black fur.

Reaching the apple tree, the bear rose on its hind legs. It lifted its giant paw to strike—

At a beehive! Kate almost laughed out loud in relief. The bear was only reaching for the beehive hanging from a branch!

The hive fell to the ground, spilling honey. Angry bees swarmed around the tree. They buzzed through the mist, darkening the orchard. One of them stung Kate on her arm. She covered the

sting with her hand and gritted her teeth. They had to get out of there!

The bear was digging its paw into the hive. Kate saw her chance. She rushed to Cloud and scrambled up onto her back. "Go!" she murmured. "Go!"

Without a backward glance, they raced away.

When she thought they had gone far enough, Kate caught her breath. "Whoa!" she told Cloud. "Slow down now."

She grinned as Cloud slowed to a walk. How well Cloud understood her!

"I wish you could be my horse, always," Kate said.

Ahead, Kate saw a wide, rushing river—the biggest one she'd ever seen in Never Land.

It must be Wough River, she thought. *The big river that runs from Torth Mountain to the sea.* Kate hadn't been there before, but she'd heard the fairies talk about it. She knew she was far, far from Pixie Hollow. It would take her ages to walk back.

That is, if I can even find my way, Kate thought. She realized she'd been wrong when she'd spoken to Vidia—she had no idea which direction Pixie Hollow was in. All the landmarks she'd passed were hidden in the fog.

For the first time since she'd left Pixie Hollow with Cloud, Kate started to feel worried. She knew she needed to find her way home as quickly as possible.

And yet she hesitated. The truth was, she wasn't ready to say good-bye to Cloud.

Cloud suddenly lifted her head. She looked alert.

"What is it?" Kate asked.

A whinny rang out from across the river. Then another. It was the herd! Kate nudged the horse with her heels.

When they reached the edge of the water, Cloud didn't even pause. The fast-moving water frothed around her hooves as she charged across. Kate couldn't tell if the river was shallow or if Cloud was actually striding across the surface.

Within moments, Cloud was scrambling up the far bank. The herd was just ahead. Kate's thoughts of returning to Pixie Hollow melted away.

Chapter 8

As the day wore on, Silvermist tried her best to follow the trails through the damp grass. But doubts constantly tugged at her mind. Sometimes the trail disappeared. Other times it seemed to go in two directions at once. And, as Mia had pointed out, were they even really following Kate? With every turn, Silvermist doubted her choices.

If only there were some way to be sure!

Once, when Silvermist peered through the fog, she thought she saw a dark-haired fairy flying fast.

"Vidia!" she called, hoping the fairy might have seen Kate. "Is that you?"

But if Vidia heard her, she didn't reply.

At last, in a valley, Silvermist lost the trail completely. She stopped and looked around. A short distance away stood a crooked old apple tree. A broken beehive lay on the ground beneath it. A few bees buzzed around the tree.

Silvermist was tired. Her wings ached. She could see that the girls were exhausted, too.

"It's useless!" Mia complained, flopping down to the ground. "Kate's on a horse. We'll never catch up with her." Her forehead furrowed. "It's just like Kate to go running off and leave us behind to worry about her."

"We can't give up," Silvermist said.

"Mia's right," Lainey agreed. "We should go back to Pixie Hollow and wait for Kate there. After all, Never Land is an island. If she goes around it, she'll end up back there eventually. Right?"

"There's a part of the legend I didn't tell you," Silvermist said. "I didn't want you to be afraid. But Kate is in danger. According to the legend, once the mist horse has a rider, it never lets her go. It will spirit her away to the clouds—forever."

The girls stared at her, wide-eyed. "That means we might never see Kate again?" Lainey whispered.

Mia leaped to her feet. "We have to go now!"

At that moment, they saw a large, dark shape coming toward them through the mist. *Not a horse,* Silvermist thought, peering at it. *Something bigger . . .*

"Bear!" Gabby gasped.

"Run!" cried Mia.

"No! Don't!" Lainey whispered. "That will make it want to chase you."

The girls froze. The bear was coming closer. It was no more than twenty feet away from them now.

"I'm scared," said Gabby.

"Somebody *do* something!" hissed Mia.

Silvermist fluttered in distress. She was only a tiny fairy! How could she stop a huge bear? Maybe she could throw an apple at it? Or should she fly right at the bear and try to distract it? She flittered back and forth, unsure what to do.

Just then, she heard a string of high-pitched squeaks. Silvermist looked around. She realized the squeaks were coming from Lainey.

The bear heard them, too. It rose onto its hind legs and sniffed the air. It seemed confused.

A moment passed. Lainey squeaked again. The bear turned and lumbered away.

The girls stayed frozen until the bear was out of sight. Then everyone whooshed

out a sigh of relief. "I didn't know you could speak Bear!" Mia said to Lainey.

"I can't," Lainey admitted. "I was speaking Mouse. I don't know why—it just came out."

"What did you say?" Gabby asked.

Lainey grinned sheepishly. "I said, 'I've lost my brothers and sisters. There are twenty more like me. Have you seen them?'"

"He probably thought you were the biggest mouse he'd ever seen," Silvermist said with a chuckle.

Everyone laughed. But their laughter quickly faded. "Is Kate going to be okay?" Gabby asked.

Lainey glanced at Silvermist with a worried look. "I hope so."

Mia was collecting apples from the tree. Suddenly, she stopped and sucked in her breath. "Look!" she said, holding an apple core up by its stem. "It's been eaten. And not by a bear."

"It could have been Kate!" Lainey said. "That means she did pass through here!"

Silvermist looked to the far end of the valley. "I think Wough River is just ahead. She'll have to stop to rest at some point. Let's hope we can catch her there."

When they reached the river, Silvermist lighted on Gabby's shoulder. They stood on the rocky bank, looking at the water rushing past. Silvermist took a deep breath and let the sound soothe her nerves. Water always made her feel calmer.

"She's not here," Mia said, looking as if she might cry. "And how will we ever get across?" The shore on the other side of the river was nearly lost in the fog.

"Hello?" came a voice from the mist.

Silvermist looked around. No one was there.

"Silvermist?"

"Did you call me?" Silvermist asked the girls.

They all shook their heads. *Am I hearing things?* wondered Silvermist.

"It's me." The fog swirled in front of Silvermist. She made out the shape of one wing, then another. Then Myka appeared. She was wearing a cottony top and pants and a cotton-ball hat. "I'm in camouflage so predators won't see me. You can't be too careful in this fog," she explained.

"Have you seen Kate?" Mia asked quickly.

Myka shook her head. "I haven't seen anyone except Vidia. And even she was on her way back to Pixie Hollow. The fog seems to be worse over here."

So it was *Vidia I saw,* thought Silvermist.

"The mist is retreating around Pixie Hollow," Myka said. "The Home Tree is all clear. Maybe that means the fog is leaving Never Land."

The girls looked stricken. "Oh no. Kate!" said Mia.

"What is it?" Myka asked.

Silvermist explained the myth to Myka. "But maybe there's still time," she said. Being near the water was helping her think more clearly. "The fog follows the mist horses. And it's as thick as we've seen it here. Perhaps that's a sign that the horses are nearby. And maybe Kate is with them."

"Do you really think so?" Lainey asked.

Silvermist took a deep breath. Even

though she'd made mistakes, she'd gotten the girls this far.

"I'm almost sure of it," she told the others.

Lainey squinted at the water. "Okay," she said slowly. "But how do we get to the other side?"

Chapter 9

The river was wide and the current strong. Silvermist knew the girls couldn't swim across. And they couldn't fly like fairies.

She looked around. Her eyes fell on the remains of an old tree that had fallen upstream. It looked almost long enough to stretch from one bank to the other.

"Maybe we could use that log as a bridge," she said.

The girls walked up to the log and strained to lift it. It didn't budge.

"Good thing I have a little extra fairy dust," said Myka. "This will lighten our load." She sprinkled the dust on the log.

"One, two, three, lift!" shouted Silvermist.

The girls raised the log easily. It stood straight up like a telephone pole.

"Now let it drop!" Silvermist cried.

They did, and the log fell across the river with a huge splash. Silvermist grinned. She'd been right about the length. The far end landed on the opposite shore.

Lainey eyed the log nervously. "It looks slippery."

"That's one thing I can help with,"

Silvermist said. Using her water magic, she drew water from the wood, drying off the top of the log. A stream of droplets trailed behind her like a banner until the tree's surface was dry.

"I'll go in front," Mia said. "Gabby, stay right behind me."

Mia stepped out onto the log. Gabby followed, flapping her arms. "If I start to fall, I can use my wings."

Mia grimaced as the log trembled. "Be careful, Gabby. Remember, some of us don't *have* wings."

"We can think of it like a balance beam," Lainey said. "Like in gymnastics class."

Silvermist had no idea what Lainey was talking about. She knew the girls went to school on the mainland. Maybe they learned how to walk on logs there.

The girls put one foot in front of the other, stepping carefully. Slowly, they made their way across.

"Look at me, Silvermist!" Gabby giggled. "I'm a balance-talent fairy!"

Mia hopped off the log, landing on the muddy bank. Laughing, Gabby leaped into her waiting arms. But as she did, her feet pushed the log away from the shore.

"Ahhh!" screamed Lainey, who hadn't quite reached the end. Her arms flailed. She began to lose her balance.

"Jump!" cried Silvermist.

Lainey leaped as the log broke free. Her feet splashed down in the water, but her hands landed in the mud on the bank. Mia and Gabby scrambled to pull her onshore.

"Are you okay?" Mia asked.

"I think so," Lainey said shakily as she climbed to her feet. She looked down at her soaked jeans and dirty shirt. "Just wet—and muddy. Yuck!" She grinned up at Mia. "I don't know how we're going to explain *this* to your parents when they wake up."

Mia grinned back, and Silvermist sighed with relief. That had been a close one.

"Do we go left, right, or straight?" Lainey asked, turning to Silvermist.

Silvermist looked around. The fog was thicker than ever to her right. She was sure now that her guess about the horses had been correct.

"Follow me!" she said.

✳

Kate's heart thudded. Cloud had climbed up and up a steep, narrow trail. They were close to the herd. That meant they were close to the end of their journey, too.

She could hear the horses, but she couldn't see them. High whinnies and low nickers echoed through the mist. The fog was so thick here, it was like walking through cotton. The ground beneath them felt thin and rocky—Kate could hear stones clattering beneath Cloud's hooves. A chilly wind was blowing.

Then, suddenly, Kate saw the herd. The horses all lifted their heads to watch Kate and Cloud's approach. In the swirling mist, the animals looked ghostly.

Cloud rode Kate into the center of the herd. The horses circled them, some of them nuzzling Cloud in greeting. An electric feeling coursed through Kate. Was this really happening to her? Even the animal-talent fairy Fawn hadn't been able to talk to the horses. And yet, Kate was being welcomed into their midst.

Kate wished this moment would never end.

But then she heard voices. Not horses, or even fairies, but human voices. At first, she couldn't make out what they were saying. Then, quite clearly, she heard her name: *"K-a-a-ate!"*

It was Mia!

Then she heard Lainey and Gabby, and small, thin fairy voices, too. They were all calling out to her.

She couldn't see her friends through the fog, so she steered Cloud toward the sound of their voices. Suddenly, Cloud stopped so fast that Kate fell forward against her mane. Cloud's front hoof dislodged a stone. Kate listened as it bounced down . . .

and down . . .

and down.

At that moment, the wind shifted, briefly clearing the mist. Kate gasped. She and Cloud stood at the edge of a narrow ledge. Before them lay a deep, rocky canyon. On the other side of the canyon were Kate's friends, separated from her by the huge chasm.

Mia, Lainey, and Gabby were waving and screaming. Now she could hear their cries more clearly.

"Get away from there, Kate! The horse is . . ."

Kate couldn't hear the rest. She tried

to get Cloud to back up, but the herd was crowded in behind them. There was nowhere to go.

Cloud took a step forward. They were going to fall!

"No!" shouted Mia.

"Stop!" cried Lainey.

"Kate!" screamed Gabby.

But it was too late. Cloud stepped off the edge.

chapter 10

Kate squeezed her eyes shut. She braced herself, expecting to drop like a stone. Instead, she felt a gentle wind against her face.

Kate opened her eyes. Cloud was galloping in the air high above the canyon. They were flying!

Cloud rode the wind. Legs pumping, she climbed up above the fog right into the clear blue sky.

Kate couldn't say a word. She was breathless with excitement. They were really and truly flying!

The other mist horses galloped around them. With a sound like rolling thunder, the herd stampeded across the sky.

At last, Kate found her voice. She cried out, a loud, joyful whoop. She felt like the queen of the sky!

Just when it seemed as if they might leave the earth for good, Cloud began to turn. The herd followed. They raced back and landed lightly on the narrow strip of land, across the chasm from where they'd come. Cloud had brought Kate to her friends.

Kate slid off the mist horse and grinned. "Did you guys see that?"

"Kate!" Mia rushed over and wrapped her in a hug. Lainey and Gabby joined her. "You're all right!"

"Of course I'm all right," said Kate, surprised. "Why wouldn't I be? And what are you all doing here anyway?"

"We thought the horse had kidnapped you!" Gabby said.

"You mean Cloud?" Kate patted the horse's neck. "Of course not. She's my new best friend."

Silvermist and the other girls explained everything—the mist horse legend, the scary thought that Kate might be spirited away, and the long journey they'd taken to find her.

"I was afraid we'd never find you, after my many wrong turns," Silvermist said.

"I even went to the beach, thinking you might be there."

"I *did* go to the beach," Kate said. "Before I went to Vine Grove."

"Silvermist, you were right all along," Lainey said.

Myka smiled at her water-talent friend. "It seems you're a better tracker than you realize."

Silvermist's glow turned pink as she blushed at the compliment. "So I guess the legend was wrong," she said. "The mist horses aren't dangerous. I wonder how that idea ever came to be."

"I'll bet I know. Maybe once upon a

time someone *did* ride away with the mist horses forever. After riding with Cloud, I can understand why they would want to." Kate laughed as Cloud nuzzled her cheek. "But I can't believe you were worried. My horse would never do anything bad."

Mia looked puzzled. "Did you just say *my* horse?"

Kate gave a sheepish smile. "I guess I did. And in a way, she is mine—like I'm hers. But just now, when we were riding, flying up in the air, I realized Cloud doesn't need a rider. She needs to be free. She needs to run wild with her herd."

Kate hugged the mist horse around the neck, holding on tightly for a long moment. Then she stepped back. "Go on now," she said. "Go be with your friends. I'll never forget you."

Cloud looked Kate in the eye and whinnied. Then she took off, climbing into the sky once again. The other horses galloped toward her. They met in a flurry of hooves and mist. Together, they raced away.

"Look!" Silvermist exclaimed. "The fog is lifting!"

The mist rose like a curtain. They could see the landscape clearly now: the cliffs, the canyons, and the ocean in the distance.

Kate, her friends, and the fairies watched the horses until all they could see were the last thin wisps of their tails trailing across the sky.

"Those clouds will be bringing rain," Silvermist added. "We should get back to the Home Tree." She winked at Gabby. "Before our wings get wet and we can't fly."

Gabby laughed. "You know I can't fly without fairy dust! Anyway, I'd rather walk with Kate." She reached for Kate's hand.

Kate squeezed Gabby's hand in her own. She was glad to be back with her friends. And in a way, she was glad to have two feet on solid ground again.

"What about you, Kate?" Silvermist asked. "Are you ready?"

Kate nodded. "I've had enough adventure for one day." She smiled at Silvermist. "Lead the way."

This is the end of

from *the*
mist

Flip the book over to read

a
dandelion
wish

The NeverGirls
Disney

a dandelion wish

*

From the Mist

Written by
Kiki Thorpe

illustrated by
Jana Christy

A STEPPING STONE BOOK™
RANDOM HOUSE 🏛 NEW YORK

For Axel and Udo
—*K.T.*

For John and Janee
—*J.C.*

randomhousekids.com/disney
ISBN 978-0-7364-3460-7
Printed in the United States of America
10 9 8 7 6 5 4 3 2 1

Never Land

Far away from the world we know, on the distant seas of dreams, lies an island called Never Land. It is a place full of magic, where mermaids sing, fairies play, and children never grow up. Adventures happen every day, and anything is possible.

There are two ways to reach Never Land. One is to find the island yourself. The other is for it to find you. Finding Never Land on your own takes a lot of luck and a pinch of fairy dust. Even then, you will only find the island if it wants to be found.

Every once in a while, Never Land drifts close to our world . . . so close a fairy's laugh slips through. And every once in an even longer while, Never Land opens its doors to a special few. Believing in magic and fairies from the bottom of your heart can make the extraordinary happen. If you suddenly hear tiny bells or feel a sea breeze where there is no sea, pay careful attention. Never Land may be close by. You could find yourself there in the blink of an eye.

One day, four special girls came to Never Land in just this way. This is their story.

Mermaid Lagoon

Pixie Hollow

Skull Rock

Torth Mountain

"All right."

Gabby thought for a moment.

"Once upon a time, there was a fairy who lived in a place called Pixie Hollow."

DISNEY

The NeVeR GiRLs

a
dandelion
wish

WritteN by
Kiki Thorpe

IllustRated by
JaNa ChRisty

A STEPPING STONE BOOK™

RANDOM HOUSE 🏠 NEW YORK

chapter 1

Mia Vasquez awoke Saturday morning with a fluttery feeling in her chest. A feeling that something great awaited her that day.

She rubbed her eyes, trying to recall what it was. Then she remembered: *Never Land.*

The two words sent her leaping from her bed. She ran to the window and looked out at the backyard. White clouds chased each other across the blue sky. The

grass was tall and the flowers bloomed in their beds. But it was the high wooden fence that held Mia's attention.

The day before, Mia, her little sister, Gabby, and her friends Kate and Lainey had discovered that by crawling through a loose board in the fence, they could reach the magical island of Never Land. No one knew how the passage between the two worlds had come to be—not even the fairies whose magic had brought the girls to Never Land in the first place. But to Mia it was a dream come true. To think she could visit the fairy world anytime she wanted, just by going through the fence in her own backyard!

Mia dressed quickly in a polka-dotted skirt and her favorite pink T-shirt. Her long, curly black hair fell

over her shoulders. She considered a pretty pair of sandals, then pulled on her sneakers instead. Sneakers were better for adventures—and there were always adventures to be had in Never Land.

When she was dressed, Mia hurried downstairs to the kitchen. She poured herself a bowl of cereal and slid into a chair next to her little sister. Gabby was wearing a pink tutu and a pair of costume fairy wings—her everyday outfit. She was drawing a picture of a fairy with crayons.

The girls' mother was standing at the kitchen counter, drinking a cup of coffee. "That's a nice drawing, Gabby," she said. "What's the fairy's name?"

"That's Tinker Bell," Gabby said. "She lives in Pixie Hollow."

Mrs. Vasquez smiled. "Where is that?"

"It's on the other side of the— Ow! Mia!" Gabby exclaimed as Mia kicked her under the table. When she caught Gabby's eye, Mia frowned and shook her head. Their parents didn't know about Never Land, and Mia didn't want them to find out. She had a feeling that if they did, the girls' adventuring would be over.

Out the kitchen window, Mia could see her father working in the yard. She hoped he would be done soon. Otherwise, they couldn't sneak through the fence.

"Is Papi going to be doing yard work for long?" Mia asked her mother casually. "Kate and Lainey are coming over. We were going to, um . . . play outside."

"Your friends can't come over today, Mia," her mother said. "I'm going out to

do some errands, and I need you to look after Gabby."

"What? But I already told them they could come!" Mia cried.

"You'll have to call them and tell them they can't," her mother replied.

And not go to Never Land? Mia couldn't bear the thought. "Can't they come over anyway?" she asked. "We can all watch Gabby together."

"No, Mia," said her mom. "If you get busy playing with your friends, you'll forget to keep an eye on Gabby."

"I wouldn't!" Mia said. She thought of the first time they'd found themselves in Never Land, pulled there on a fairy's blink. Hadn't she and her friends taken good care of Gabby then? But, of course, she couldn't point this out to her mother.

"Kate and Lainey can come over another time," Mrs. Vasquez said.

"It's not fair!" Mia complained. "Papi's here. Why can't he watch Gabby?"

"Papi is busy today. Mia, please don't sulk. It's just one day. You're old enough to be responsible."

"Who cares about being responsible?" Mia grumbled under her breath. She watched, arms folded, as her mother picked up her purse and left.

When she was gone, Mia called Kate and Lainey and told them they couldn't come over. Then she returned to the table, plopped herself down in a chair, and glared at her sister.

Gabby didn't seem to notice. "Do you want to play a game?"

"No," Mia snapped.

"Do you want to color?" asked Gabby.

Mia's frown deepened. "No. Why don't you go watch TV or something?"

"I'm not supposed to watch TV unless Mami says it's okay," Gabby pointed out.

"Well, I'm in charge today, and *I* say it's okay," Mia replied.

At once, Gabby hopped up from the table. She ran into the living room. A moment later, Mia heard the TV turn on.

With nothing better to do, Mia followed her into the living room. She flopped down on the sofa. On the television screen, a bunch of cartoon monsters were singing a silly song.

Mia sighed. She couldn't think of anything more frustrating than to be stuck watching a lame kiddie show when she could be spending time with *real* fairies.

She looked out the living room window
at the high wooden fence. Never Land lay
just on the other side. She could reach it
in less than thirty seconds.

Well, why shouldn't I? Mia thought. *I could
just pop over and see what's going on in Pixie Hollow.
I'll be back before anyone even knows I'm gone.*

Mia glanced at her sister. Gabby was

caught up in her cartoon. *She'll be fine for a few minutes,* Mia thought.

Quietly, she slipped off the couch and let herself out the back door.

She didn't see her father, but she could hear him whistling. He was working somewhere around the side of the house. Now was her chance.

The loose board was on the fence that separated the yard from their neighbor's. Mia had to spend a few moments nudging the boards until she found the right one. The board swung sideways on its nail, creating a gap just big enough for her to squeeze through.

As Mia knelt down, she felt a warm breeze on her face. She could smell jasmine and sun-warmed moss—the sweet scent of Pixie Hollow. She took a deep breath, then

crawled through the opening, pulling the board back into place behind her.

*

She came out from a hollow tree into a sun-dappled forest. To her left was a wildflower-filled meadow. To her right, Havendish Stream burbled between its banks. And just beyond the stream lay Pixie Hollow. Mia could see fairies darting through the air as they flew to and from the giant Home Tree.

Mia heard a commotion downstream. She followed the sound around a bend, to a small wooden bridge. Dozens of fairies swarmed around the bridge. They carried rope and bits of wood and buckets full of sand.

Mia saw Tinker Bell flying past. "Hi, Tink. What's going on?" she asked.

"The footbridge is out," Tink replied. Now Mia saw that part of the bridge had collapsed into the stream. "We think Bingo must have smashed it when he was chasing fairies."

"Oh no!" Bingo was Mia's cat. The day before, he'd slipped through the fence into Never Land and caused trouble. "Can you fix it?"

"Yes, but it will take a lot of work," Tink said happily. "I'd better get back." She waved to Mia and flew off. Tink was always happiest when she had something to fix.

The fairies at the bridge all seemed busy, so Mia decided to go to the Home Tree. Perhaps she could find someone to talk to there.

In the pebbled courtyard, Mia saw

sweeping-talent fairies tidying up. They waved to Mia, but kept on with their jobs. It was the same in the kitchen. When Mia peered through the tiny doorway, the cooking- and baking-talent fairies barely looked up.

"Busy day in Pixie Hollow," said the baking fairy Dulcie as she rolled out pie dough. "Lots of hungry fairies to feed."

Mia was disappointed. She'd hoped she might come upon a tea party or a game of fairy tag. But everyone in Pixie Hollow was hard at work. Mia wondered if she should help—after all, it was her cat that had caused the mess. But she knew she shouldn't leave Gabby alone for too long. Time worked differently in Never Land, and Mia couldn't be sure if a minute or an hour had gone by since she had left.

As Mia started back, she passed a tiny house made from a gourd that sat on one of the Home Tree's lowest branches. She tapped on the little wooden door with her finger.

The garden fairy Rosetta opened the door. She was dressed in a glorious ruffled gown made from a pink carnation. "Mia!" Rosetta exclaimed. "I was hoping someone might drop by. I'm glad it's you!"

"Are you going to a party?" Mia asked hopefully, eyeing Rosetta's fancy dress.

Rosetta sighed sadly. "No parties today—not even a picnic. Everyone is too busy cleaning up after . . . well, you know, what happened with Bingo."

"Why aren't you busy, too?" asked Mia.

"Well, Bingo made a great mess of almost everything, but he left all the

flowers alone. There's not much for a garden fairy to do. So I've been trying on dresses. Sometimes I do that when I'm feeling bored," Rosetta admitted. "But now I'm out of dresses—I've tried on everything!"

Suddenly, Mia had an idea. It was such a good idea that she wondered why she hadn't thought of it before. "Why don't you come to my house? I have lots of dresses that would fit you perfectly," she said, thinking of her doll clothes.

"You mean, go through the fig tree to the mainland? I don't know." Rosetta suddenly looked nervous. "Some fairies say it's dangerous."

Mia laughed. "It's not dangerous. I just came through it! Rosetta, you have to come. I have a pink velvet dress that would look beautiful on you. Oh! And

one made of blue lace. And a green one with a little matching bag . . ."

As Mia described the dresses, Rosetta's blue eyes widened. At last, she burst out, "I'd love to see them all!"

"Come on. Let's go right now," said Mia.

With Rosetta flying beside her, Mia led the way back to the hollow tree. She was thrilled. This was the perfect answer to her problem. She could look after Gabby and still have fun!

But when they got to the tree, Rosetta hesitated. "Are you sure it's safe?" she asked.

"You can ride in my pocket, if it makes you feel better," Mia said.

Rosetta flew into Mia's pocket. Then Mia crawled into the hollow tree, and back to her own world.

Chapter 2

As Mia came back through the fence into her yard, she could still hear her father whistling from somewhere around the side of the house. *Good,* Mia thought. That meant she'd only been gone for a few moments.

Quickly, Mia crossed the yard and went in the back door to the house. "I'll be in my room, Gabby," she said as she passed the living room.

Gabby looked up from the TV. "What's that?" she asked, eyeing the lump in Mia's pocket.

"Nothing. Mind your own business," Mia said, hurrying up the stairs to her room.

In the hallway, Bingo was prowling. When he saw Mia, he wrapped himself around her legs and purred. Inside Mia's pocket, Rosetta tensed.

"Go away, Bingo." Mia nudged the cat gently with her foot. She slipped past him into her room, quickly shutting the door behind her. On the other side, Bingo yowled in protest.

"It's okay," Mia said to Rosetta. "You can come out now."

Rosetta wriggled out of the pocket. "Phew!" She fluffed her long red hair.

Then her eyes widened, and she gave a little gasp. "Oh my!"

Mia glanced around, seeing her room through Rosetta's eyes. Instantly, she regretted not making her bed that morning. And all those clothes on the floor—why hadn't she noticed them until now?

Mia hastily scooped up socks and T-shirts, throwing them in the hamper, and yanked the purple coverlet up over her bed. But when Mia glanced back at Rosetta, she realized the fairy wasn't looking at the mess. She was staring, transfixed, at the corner of the room, where a large dollhouse stood.

Rosetta flew over and landed in the dollhouse's living room. She examined the little sofa, the miniature grandfather

clock, and the postage-stamp pictures on the walls. Her fairy glow cast a warm light over the small room, making it look as if the dollhouse lamps were lit.

Moving from room to room, Rosetta explored the rest of the dollhouse. She touched the tiny china teacups in the dining room. She opened the oven door in the kitchen. She even stretched out on the canopy bed in the guest bedroom.

Mia's breath caught in delight. She had always liked playing with her dollhouse, but it had never been more than a pretty toy. The moment the fairy stepped inside, though, the house came to life.

"Who lives here?" Rosetta asked.

"No one," Mia replied. "It's . . . just for fun."

"Just for fun?" Rosetta cried in surprise. "But it's a perfect home for a fairy!"

Mia grinned, imagining a fairy living in her dollhouse.

At that moment, the door to Mia's room burst open. Gabby stood in the doorway. "I knew it!" she crowed, spying Rosetta. "I knew you had a fairy here!"

"Gabby!" cried Mia. "You're supposed to knock!"

Gabby ignored her. She barged into the room. "What are you guys playing? Can I play, too? Will you come to my room, Rosetta? I want to show you my toys and my books and my stuffed animals. Can you come right now? Can you?"

Mia grabbed hold of her sister by one wing and spun her around. "Out!" she exclaimed. "Get out of my room!"

"Let go, Mia!" Gabby shouted.

"It's all right, Mia," Rosetta said. She flew out of the dollhouse, which became just an ordinary toy once again.

"No, it's not," Mia said. "It's my room, and I didn't invite Gabby in. She's *intruding.*" Mia knew she was being mean, but she couldn't stop herself. Gabby was the reason she was stuck at home and not in Never Land. Even though Mia knew it wasn't Gabby's fault, she couldn't help being mad at her.

As the sisters glared at each other, a blur of brown fur streaked into the room through the open door.

"Bingo!" the girls shrieked. They dove for the cat at the same time. Their heads collided with a loud smack. Bingo shot past them, headed right for Rosetta.

The fairy screamed and darted into the air. Bingo leaped onto Mia's dresser. He stood on his hind legs, batting the air as he tried to reach the fairy.

Gabby jumped up to grab him, but she wasn't quite tall enough. Instead, she knocked Mia's jewelry box off the dresser. The box crashed to the floor, and the hinges broke. All the trinkets inside scattered.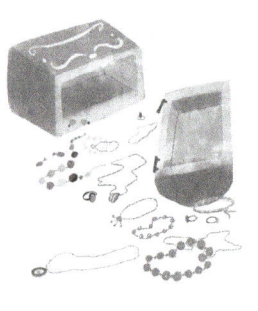

"Gabby!" Mia wailed. "Bingo!" She didn't know who to yell at first. She snatched the cat off her dresser and tucked him under her arm. Then she clamped her other hand down on Gabby's shoulder, steering her toward the door. "Both of you—out!"

"I want to stay!" Gabby said, digging in her heels.

"No. You mess up *everything*," Mia said. She pushed Gabby and Bingo into the hall and locked the door behind them.

"Fine! Then I'll do something fun in *my* room. And *you're* not invited!" Gabby shouted through the door.

"Fine with me!" Mia shouted back.

Gabby stomped away. A second later, Mia heard her bedroom door slam.

"I don't think she meant to let Bingo in," Rosetta said, fluttering down from the ceiling.

Mia touched her head. It throbbed where she'd run into Gabby. "You don't know what it's like to have a little sister," she told Rosetta. "Gabby's always getting in the way."

"Maybe I should go home," the fairy said. She looked nervous, and Mia realized she was still afraid of Bingo.

"Don't leave yet!" Mia begged. If Rosetta left now, the whole day would be ruined. "I haven't even shown you the dresses!"

Mia hurried to her closet and pulled out the two shoe boxes where she kept her doll clothes. She lifted the lids and began laying the dresses out one by one.

Pink, yellow, green, gold. Satin, taffeta, and lace. Some of the dresses were trimmed with ribbon. Others were bursting with petticoats. Still others had matching cloaks and hats.

Rosetta came closer, lured by the lovely clothes. "Look how many there are!"

"Try one on," Mia urged.

"All right. Just one." After much

consideration, Rosetta selected a ruffled
pink dress with a gold sash.

The dress fit perfectly. Rosetta flew
back and forth in front of Mia's dresser
mirror, admiring herself. Mia clapped
her hands. The dress had never looked
this pretty on her dolls. "Try this one

next!" she urged, holding up a yellow ball gown.

Rosetta tried on dress after dress. Mia thought each one looked lovelier than the last. She was having so much fun she didn't notice the time passing.

Bang! Bang! Bang! A pounding sound from outside startled Mia.

"What was that?" asked Rosetta.

"I don't know." Suddenly, Mia thought of Gabby. How long had it been since she'd seen her? "I'll be right back," she told Rosetta.

Mia went across the hall. But Gabby's room was empty. Downstairs, the television was still on, but Gabby wasn't watching. She wasn't in the kitchen or the bathroom, either.

Mia went back to her room. "I can't find her," she told Rosetta.

"Who?" asked the fairy. She had on a green satin dress and was admiring herself in the mirror.

"Gabby!" exclaimed Mia. "She's not anywhere in the house."

Rosetta looked at her. "Where else could she be?"

With a sinking feeling, Mia suddenly knew exactly where her sister was. Gabby had gone through the fence into Pixie Hollow.

"Gabby, you're such a pest," she grumbled to herself. But she hurried down the stairs. It was one thing for Mia to go to Never Land on her own. But Gabby was just a little girl. Who knew

what kind of trouble she could get into?

When she stepped outside, Mia spotted Gabby's sweatshirt, the one she'd been wearing that morning. It was lying on the ground near the fence. Mia knew then that she was right. Gabby must have taken it off right before she went through the hole.

Mia saw her father standing at the fence. He had a hammer in his hand. But what was he doing?

As Mia watched, her father brought the hammer down on the fence. *Bang! Bang! Bang!*

"Oh no!" Mia cried. Her father was fixing the hole in the fence—and Gabby was on the other side!

Chapter 3

Iridessa, a light-talent fairy, knelt before a pool of sunlight. She reached into the pool and pulled out a sunbeam. Her hands shaped the sunbeam into a ball, like a golden glowing pearl. Then she placed it in her basket.

Iridessa sat back on her heels and eyed the basket of sunbeams. It was almost full. *Is that enough?* she wondered.

Better get a few more, she decided. In Iridessa's opinion, it was always better to

be safe than sorry. With the bridge builders working through the night, Pixie Hollow would need extra light.

As soon as she was done collecting sunbeams, she needed to round up more fireflies. There was so much to do! Luckily, Iridessa had made a plan for the day. She glanced up at the sun high in the sky and smiled. She was right on schedule.

Iridessa reached into the pool again. But just as her fingers touched it, a shadow fell over her. She turned.

A giant loomed above. Iridessa noticed that it had wings—and a tutu. "Gabby?" she said.

"Hi, Iridessa." The girl squatted down next to her. "Will you come to my room? I'm having a party."

"Now?" Iridessa wondered why anyone would have a party at such a busy time.

"Everyone is invited—except Mia," Gabby told her.

Suddenly, Iridessa understood. "Did you have a fight with your sister?"

Gabby's forehead furrowed. "She won't let me play with her and Rosetta. And

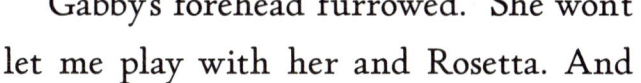

she yelled at me, even though it wasn't my fault about Bingo. And she made me leave. She pulled my wings! She's mean!"

Iridessa didn't know what to make of all this. But she did know what it was like to be mad at someone. "Perhaps she wasn't mean on purpose," she said.

"She was so," said Gabby. "I never want to see her again."

"Come now," said Iridessa. "There must be something you like about your sister."

Gabby shook her head.

"Think hard," Iridessa urged. "Just one thing."

Gabby considered. "Well, sometimes she lets me watch TV."

"What is that?" asked the fairy.

Gabby looked at her in amazement. "It's . . . TV!"

Some quaint Clumsy custom, no doubt, thought Iridessa. "Well, imagine if you didn't have your sister *or* TV. Wouldn't that be sad?"

"I guess so," said Gabby.

"I'll bet if you remind Mia how much you like it when you watch TV, it will make her feel happy. And then you two can make up," Iridessa said.

"Do you really think so?" Gabby asked.

"Yes," said Iridessa. "People always like to hear good things about themselves. Sometimes the best way to get over an argument is to remember the nice things about each other. You should talk to Mia. Come on, I'll take you back to the hollow tree."

Iridessa picked up her basket of sunbeams. This wasn't part of her day's plan.

35

But she was glad to help. Iridessa liked to see things sorted out. And it had only taken her—Iridessa glanced at the sun—forty-seven seconds!

She led Gabby across the meadow, back to the tree that held the portal to the girls' world. Iridessa stopped at the entrance to the hollow.

"Fly safely," she said, in the fairy manner.

"Okay." Gabby turned and ducked into the hollow. A second later, she came right back out.

"What's wrong?" Iridessa asked.

"The hole isn't there," said Gabby.

"Of course it is," Iridessa replied. "You came through it earlier, didn't you?"

Gabby nodded. "But now it's gone."

Iridessa thought Gabby must be mistaken. She set down her basket and flew into the tree. It was dark inside the hollow, but all fairies glow a little and Iridessa's glow was stronger than most. She could see the inside walls of the hollow, smooth and unbroken.

"It's gone! The portal's gone!" Iridessa exclaimed, flying out of the tree.

"I told you," said Gabby.

"What should I do?" Iridessa asked. This was important news! But whether it was good or bad news, Iridessa wasn't certain. She fluttered back and forth. She sometimes got flustered when things didn't work out as planned.

Just then, a messenger-talent fairy flew by. Iridessa zipped over and told her

what they'd discovered. Within moments, the messenger spread the news around Pixie Hollow. Fairies and sparrow men all stopped what they were doing. They came to examine the tree.

"So it's true?" asked Queen Clarion, flying up.

"It is," said Tinker Bell, who'd been inspecting the tree. "The hollow is still there. But the portal has vanished!"

As the fairies buzzed with the news, Iridessa's eyes darted to Gabby. The girl stood off to the side, watching the fairies silently. She seemed to be waiting to be told what to do. The other fairies barely noticed her, however. They were all focused on the tree.

Iridessa flew over to Queen Clarion. "What about Gabby?" she murmured.

"She can't get home. Someone will need to look after her."

The queen rubbed a hand across her forehead. She looked distracted. "Yes, you're right, of course. That's very good of you, Iridessa."

"What? Oh! No." Iridessa shook her head and tried to explain. "That's not what I meant. . . ." But the queen was already flying away.

Iridessa sighed. She had sunbeams to collect and fireflies to gather. Looking after a Clumsy was *not* part of her plan.

She flew back over to Gabby. "Don't worry," she said brightly. "I'm sure the hole will open again in no time." Iridessa wasn't sure of any such thing. But she didn't want Gabby to worry.

In the meantime, she had no choice. If she was going to stick to her plan, she'd just have to bring Gabby along with her.

Well, she's only a young girl, after all, she thought. *How hard can it be to look after her?*

chapter 4

Mia ran toward her father, crying, "Papi, wait!"

Mr. Vasquez looked up. "Mia?"

When she reached the fence, Mia ran her fingers along it. None of the boards budged. "There was a loose board!"

"I know, I fixed it," her father replied. "I've been meaning to repair this old fence for ages. You don't know what might get through a hole like that. Stray dogs or cats or— Mia, honey, what's the matter?"

"Gabby is . . ." Mia trailed off, her mind racing.

What if she told her father about Never Land? What would happen? Would he tell other grown-ups about the fairy world? Would he leave the hole sealed up for good? Would he even believe her?

Mia didn't know. But one thing was certain—if her parents found out she'd lost track of Gabby, she was going to be in big trouble.

Her father frowned. "Gabby is what?"

"Sleeping," Mia said quickly, making a decision. "She's taking a nap. I was afraid the hammering would wake her up."

"Well, I'm done here." Her father picked up his tools. "I've got some work to do in the garage. *Quiet* work," he added

with a wink. Then he patted Mia's cheek. "You're a good big sister."

A guilty lump rose in Mia's throat. She swallowed hard, forcing it down. *It's not my fault,* Mia told herself. *If Gabby hadn't left without telling me, this wouldn't have happened!*

When her father was gone, Mia turned back to the fence. She tried wiggling the wooden boards. She tried kicking them. Not one of them budged.

"Stupid fence!" Mia exclaimed, giving it an extra kick.

"Mia?" said a voice behind her.

Mia turned and saw Rosetta hovering. She was still wearing the green satin doll dress. "What's going on?" the fairy asked.

Gabby wasn't the only one who was trapped in the wrong world, Mia realized. Rosetta was stuck, too!

But unlike Gabby, Rosetta had magic. Maybe she could help. "Papi fixed the fence. But Gabby is in Never Land, and now she can't get home!" Mia explained. "Can you do something?"

"You mean, the way back to Never Land is gone?" Rosetta's face turned pale. Her eyelids fluttered. Mia stuck out her hand just in time to catch her as she fainted.

✻

Inside the house, Mia ran a washrag under the kitchen tap. Carefully, she squeezed a drop of water onto Rosetta's forehead.

The fairy spluttered and sat up. When she saw Mia's giant face hovering over her, she screamed.

"Sorry!" Mia backed away quickly. "I didn't mean to scare you."

Rosetta put a hand to her cheek. "What happened?"

"You fainted when I told you we can't get back to Never Land," Mia said.

Rosetta looked like she might faint again, so Mia made her comfortable on a dry kitchen sponge.

"That's better. A cup of tea would be nice, too," Rosetta said.

Mia didn't know how to make tea. But she wanted Rosetta to feel better. She fetched a doll's teacup from her room and put a drop of soda in it, then handed it to the fairy.

Rosetta took one sip and yelped. "It burns! But it's cold!"

"It's root beer," said Mia.

Rosetta drained her cup and smacked her lips. "Have you got a little something

to go with it? A poppy-seed thimblecake, perhaps? With a dollop of fresh cream and a sprinkle of pollen?"

Mia studied the cupboard. "We have crackers."

As she handed one to Rosetta, the doorbell rang. Mia ran to answer it. Her best friend, Kate McCrady, was standing on the doorstep. Mia had called Kate and Lainey for help. She remembered what

her mother had said about not having her friends over. But this was an emergency.

"You said to come over. Then you said not to come over. Then you said, 'Come over—and hurry!' Make up your mind, Mia!" Kate joked.

Mia didn't feel like laughing. She led Kate into the kitchen. Rosetta was still sitting on the counter, making her way through an  oyster cracker.

"What are you doing here?" Kate cried when she saw Rosetta. "Aren't we going to Never Land today?"

"Well, that's the thing. . . ." Mia started to explain how Rosetta had ended up on the mainland. But right away Kate interrupted.

"Wait a minute. You mean, you went

to Never Land *without* me?" Kate looked both annoyed and envious.

"Don't be mad, Kate," Mia pleaded. "I've got a big problem. Gabby is stuck in Never Land!"

"She went, too? So much for sticking with your friends," Kate grumbled.

To Mia's relief, the doorbell rang again. This time it was Lainey Winters. Her blond hair was uncombed and her glasses were slightly crooked on her face. "I came as fast as I could," she said breathlessly.

The girls listened as Mia explained how Gabby had come to be trapped in Never Land, and Rosetta stuck in their world.

"Can't you do anything?" Lainey asked Rosetta. "I mean, with fairy magic?"

"Nope, I already asked," Mia told her.

Rosetta lifted her chin. "I'm a garden fairy," she said proudly. "Holes aren't one of my talents. Our magic is different. I can make any flower bloom. I can hear the secrets inside a seed."

Kate rolled her eyes. "A lot of good that will do us."

"You said your dad nailed the board shut," Lainey said, thinking. "So really all we need to do is loosen it again."

"It's nailed down tight," Mia said. "But we can try."

The group hurried outside to study the fence. "Which board was it?" Rosetta asked.

"It was somewhere in the middle," said Mia.

"I thought it was closer to the right," said Kate.

"How can you tell?" asked Lainey. "They all look the same!"

Kate folded her arms across her chest. "Mia should know. *She* was the last one through it," she said, giving Mia a meaningful look.

"Kate, I said I was sorry!" Mia wailed.

"Actually, you didn't," Kate replied.

Mia sighed. "I'm sorry I went to Never Land without you. Will you please stop being mad now?"

"Maybe," Kate said with a smile. She kicked at a few fence boards. "Well, since we can't remember which board it is, I guess we're just going to have to try them all."

"You mean, loosen every board?" Mia was horrified. "What are my parents going to think?"

"What are they going to think when you tell them Gabby sneaked off to the magical island of Never Land while you were supposed to be watching her?" Kate asked pointedly. "Mia, it's the only way."

"Fine." Mia scowled. "I can't wait to get Gabby back . . . so I can yell at her."

Kate knelt down and began to wiggle a board. "It's really nailed tight. Ow!" She jerked back her hand. "I got a splinter."

Rosetta fluttered over to her. "Let me see it."

"Do you have healing magic?" Kate asked, holding out her thumb.

"No, but I have tiny hands." Rosetta landed on Kate's palm and began to gently work out the splinter.

That gave Mia an idea. "I know! We need something to pull the nails out." She

ran into the house and returned a few moments later with a hammer.

Using the claw end of the hammer, Mia began to wiggle the nail from the wood. "Just a little more . . . there!" Mia pulled out the nail, then pushed the board to one side, just enough so she could peek through. "I see flowers. And I can hear water running."

"That must be Havendish Stream!" Rosetta cried joyously. "Oh, I'll be back in time for tea!" She zipped right past Mia and through the gap in the fence.

At that moment, a large shape crossed in front of the gap, blocking Mia's view. She heard someone grumbling. But it didn't sound like a fairy's voice. It sounded like a grown-up.

That's not Pixie Hollow! Mia realized with a gasp. It was her neighbor Mrs. Peavy's yard—and that large shape blocking her view was Mrs. Peavy herself. Rosetta had flown right into the old woman's garden!

"What's wrong, Mia?" Kate asked behind her.

"We got the wrong board." Mia put her eye back to the crack, but she couldn't see the fairy. "Rosetta, come back!" she whispered.

There was no reply.

Mia watched through the crack. She could see Mrs. Peavy's feet. The old woman stood still for a long time. She seemed to be looking at something.

Mia's heart beat faster. Had Mrs. Peavy found Rosetta?

The old woman turned and walked back toward her house.

As soon as she was gone, Mia whispered louder, "Rosetta, are you okay?"

Silence.

Mia felt panic rising in her chest. "We have to go in there!" she cried. "Something happened to Rosetta!"

Chapter 5

"What do you know about spotting fireflies?" Iridessa asked Gabby.

The two were making their way through the forest just outside Pixie Hollow. Iridessa flew in front of Gabby, leading the way through the moss-covered trees.

"They have lights in their bottoms," Gabby replied.

"That's right," said Iridessa. "But they can be hard to see in the daytime. That's

why we need a plan. We should start by looking for puddles. Then we move on to shady thickets. Then we'll go— Are you listening, Gabby? Gabby?"

Iridessa turned. The little girl had vanished.

Iridessa hovered, looking around. *She's ten times the size of a fairy,* she thought. *How is it possible that I've lost her already?*

"BOO!" Gabby yelled, springing up from behind a bush. Iridessa was so startled that she fell from the air. She landed in a giant fern.

Gabby giggled. "I scared you!"

Iridessa could barely conceal her annoyance. "Gabby, we don't have time for games. Just stay close, now."

This time Iridessa flew behind so she could keep an eye on Gabby. But it wasn't easy. The little girl was all over the place! She'd stop to admire a fuzzy caterpillar. Then suddenly, she'd dash off to examine a mushroom or peek into a hollow log.

"It's harder than herding a butterfly!" Iridessa groaned.

Before she could stop her, Gabby darted away again. In an instant, she had vanished among the trees.

At last, Iridessa spotted the tips of Gabby's wings poking out from behind a mossy oak. "What are you up to now?" she asked, flying over.

Gabby was holding a silver dandelion. Iridessa watched as she closed her eyes and blew away all the seeds with a single breath. Ever since they'd entered the forest, Gabby had stopped to pick every

dandelion she'd seen. It was starting to drive Iridessa crazy.

"Why do you do that?" she asked.

"For a wish," Gabby said.

"On a dandelion?" Iridessa had never heard of such a thing.

"When you wish on a dandelion, a fairy hears your wish and makes it come true," Gabby replied. "That's what Mia says."

Iridessa frowned. Never fairies didn't grant wishes. In Iridessa's opinion, *planning* was how you went about making sure things turned out as you wanted. *What a lot of silly ideas Clumsies have,* she thought.

Suddenly, Gabby's eyes lit up. "Ooh, look! A firefly!" She pointed at a glimmer of light ahead in the trees.

A single firefly wasn't worth the trouble of chasing, Iridessa thought. But Gabby was already darting after it. "It's not— Wait! Come back!" Iridessa cried.

Gabby scrambled over rocks and under branches, grabbing for the firefly that was always out of reach. Iridessa was surprised at how fast the girl could run. She could barely keep up.

In moments, they were deep in the woods. The trees grew close together. But it wasn't just the trees blocking out the light—the whole forest seemed to be growing darker, almost as if night was coming on.

That can't be right, Iridessa thought. *Sunset is hours away.*

She glanced up at the sky. Between the towering trees, she could see thunderheads

gathering. Storms were rare in Never Land. But they did happen.

Suddenly, Iridessa felt worried. She put on a burst of speed to catch up with Gabby. "Don't go so far. We need to . . ."

Iridessa trailed off, forgetting the rest of her thought. Gabby was standing in the center of a clearing, surrounded by thousands of fireflies. They wove patterns in the air around her. The little girl danced with joy.

Iridessa lived in an enchanted world, but even to her, the scene was like magic. She'd never seen so many fireflies glowing 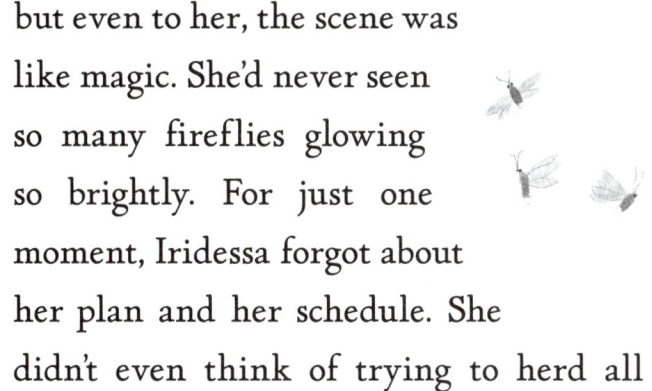 so brightly. For just one moment, Iridessa forgot about her plan and her schedule. She didn't even think of trying to herd all

the fireflies. Instead, she flew up next to Gabby. Together, they laughed and danced as the fireflies swirled around them.

Then, all at once, the lights winked out.

"What happened?" Gabby asked.

"Something scared them off," Iridessa replied, looking around.

CRRACK! There came a clap of thunder so loud Iridessa felt it in her bones. The sky opened up, and rain poured down. It came so hard and fast that it washed Iridessa right out of the air.

The fairy landed hard on the muddy ground. She tried to stand and run for shelter. But before she could, a rivulet of water picked her up and swept her away.

Iridessa bounced over the ground, carried by the water. She grabbed at roots and blades of grass, trying to hold on. But the

water tore her off. It swept up everything in its path. Leaves and sticks slammed against her. The forest spun above her. She was going to drown!

Suddenly, a hand grabbed her roughly and lifted her into the air. Iridessa found herself looking into a pair of wide brown eyes.

"Gabby!" Iridessa was so relieved she could have cried.

"Are you okay?" the girl asked.

Iridessa nodded. She was muddy and bruised. Her wings were too wet to fly. But she wasn't badly hurt.

Cradling Iridessa in her hands, Gabby ducked under a giant fern. They waited out the storm. It didn't last long. Almost as quickly as it had come, the rain cleared up.

Iridessa fanned her wet wings, trying to dry them. "We'd better go back to Pixie Hollow before we get caught in another storm," she told Gabby. "You'll have to carry me for now. I can't fly with wet wings."

"Okay," said Gabby. "Which way do we go?"

"This way." Iridessa pointed into the trees. "No . . . that doesn't look right. Is it this way?" She spun in a circle. But each way she turned, the trees looked the same.

With a sinking feeling, Iridessa realized they were lost.

chapter 6

"Are you sure about this, Kate?" Lainey asked.

Kate was using the hammer to work another nail loose from the fence board. "How else are we going to get into the garden to find Rosetta?" she asked.

"We could ring Mrs. Peavy's doorbell," Lainey suggested. "We could say we lost a ball in her yard."

"She'll never let us in," Mia said. "She doesn't even answer the door for

trick-or-treaters. On Halloween, she turns off all the lights and closes her drapes."

"I heard she's a witch," Lainey whispered.

"I heard that, too," said Mia.

Kate frowned. "I thought witches were supposed to love Halloween." She pulled the nail out. Pushing the board sideways made a gap just big enough to squeeze through.

The girls all looked at each other. "Who's going?" asked Kate. For the first time in her life, she didn't look eager to have an adventure.

"Let's do rock-paper-scissors," Mia suggested. "On the count of three. One . . . two . . . three!"

Mia scissored her fingers. Kate and Lainey both curled their fists into rocks.

Mia swallowed hard. "Okay," she said. "Wish me luck."

"Good luck," said Lainey.

"Don't get turned into a frog," said Kate.

Mia scowled at her, then crawled through the fence.

She found herself in an overgrown garden. The grass grew a foot high and the flower beds were choked with weeds. The few flowers that remained were wilted, and the herbs had all gone to seed. The sole tree in the garden was so strangled by ivy that Mia couldn't see an inch of its bark.

It sure looks *like a witch's garden,* Mia thought. She glanced up at the house, but the shades were drawn. Was it possible that Rosetta was trapped inside?

Mia tiptoed farther into the garden.

Just then, she spotted her friend. The fairy was crouched beside a bedraggled rosebush. It looked as if she was talking to it.

Mia hurried over. "There you are! We thought something happened to you. We were so worried!"

Rosetta looked up at her with tears in her eyes. "Mia, look at this place. Who would do this to a garden? Flowers need love and care. You can't just *ignore* them."

Mia was getting anxious. Mrs. Peavy could come back any minute. "We should go now," she whispered.

"But, Mia," Rosetta said, widening her eyes. "I can't *leave* them like this!"

"You there!" a gravelly voice rang out, making Mia's blood run cold. "What are you doing in my garden?"

Mia turned and saw Mrs. Peavy standing a few feet away. The woman was wearing a wide-brimmed hat that cast a shadow over the top half of her face, so Mia couldn't see her eyes. But her mouth was turned down in a deep frown. She gripped a gardening trowel in her fist as if it were a weapon.

Mia's lips moved, but no words came out. They seemed to be stuck in her throat.

"Speak up!" Mrs. Peavy came closer. Now Mia could see her eyes. They were a startling shade of blue.

"Who were you talking to?" the woman snapped. "And don't lie to me. I can smell a lie a mile away."

Is that why her nose is so long? Mia wondered. *For smelling lies?* It seemed like something a witch might be able to do. Mia decided not to take any chances. "I was talking to a fairy," she answered honestly.

"A fairy?" Mrs. Peavy made a sour face. "What nonsense!"

"But it's true!" Mia said. "She's right here!"

"What nonsense!" the woman repeated. "You must be a very silly girl."

"It's no use talking to her," Rosetta said, flying up next to Mia. "Most grown-ups can't see me. You can't see fairies if you don't believe in them."

How sad, Mia thought, *not to be able to see magic even when it's right in front of your eyes.* Suddenly, Mrs. Peavy didn't seem like a

witch. She just seemed like a lonely old woman. A very *grouchy* lonely old woman.

"Now," Mrs. Peavy was saying, "what are you going to do about my hollyhocks?"

She pointed at the fence, where a row of unkempt hollyhocks grew. Mia saw that where she'd come through, she'd knocked over a few of the tall flowers. "You'll have to pay for them," her neighbor said.

"But I don't have any money!" Mia exclaimed.

"Then you'll have to work it off," said Mrs. Peavy, folding her arms.

Moments later, Mia found herself kneeling on the ground, pulling up weeds in Mrs. Peavy's garden. "This is terrible!" Mia whispered to Rosetta. "It will take a hundred years to weed this garden. We're

never going to find Gabby. Or get you home again."

"This is my fault," said Rosetta. "If only she would go away!" She frowned at Mrs. Peavy, who was sitting on the patio, watching Mia like a hawk.

"You missed a spot!" the old woman called as the phone inside her home started to ring. She got up to answer it.

"It's about time!" Rosetta declared. Without wasting another moment, she began to fly in circles. As she did, the garden started to change.

Weeds shrank. Leaves sprouted. Brown grass turned green again. Wilted flowers straightened and burst into bloom. Round and round Rosetta went, leaving a trail of beauty in her wake. When the entire garden had been transformed,

Rosetta flew back to Mia. "There," she said, dusting off her hands. "That's much better."

Just then, Mrs. Peavy returned from the house. "I hope you've been pulling up weeds, not— What on earth?"

She froze at the sight of her beautiful garden and Mia standing in its midst.

"I'm finished, Mrs. Peavy," Mia said cheerily. When the woman didn't reply, she added, "I'll just let myself out the gate."

Mia left her neighbor staring in awe, the frown at last wiped clear off her face.

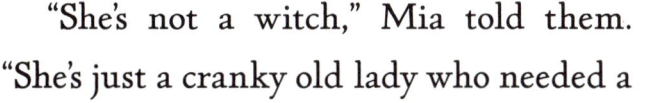

chapter 7

When Mia and Rosetta returned to the house, they found Kate and Lainey still waiting in the backyard. Lainey was biting her nails. Kate was pacing the length of the fence like a tiger in a zoo.

"What took you so long?" Lainey cried when she saw them.

"We thought for sure the witch got you," Kate added.

"She's not a witch," Mia told them. "She's just a cranky old lady who needed a

little bit of magic." She looked at Rosetta, who winked.

"While you were gone, we found something," Lainey reported. She pointed at one of the fence boards. "The nails here are a different color. They're new!"

"It must be the board your dad fixed," Kate explained. "That means it's the one that leads to Pixie Hollow!"

"Good work, guys," Mia said, picking up the hammer. She felt bad to be undoing her father's work. But what other choice did she have?

Mia was just working the hammer under the edge of the nail when the growl of a lawn mower made her jump. She turned to see her father pushing their mower around the side of the house.

Rosetta clapped her hands over her

ears. "What is that thing? It's louder than a bullfrog with a bellyache!"

"A lawn mower!" Kate shouted back. "It's for cutting the grass!"

Rosetta made a face. "All that fuss? Over a lawn's haircut?"

"Mia!" her father yelled. He said something else, but the sound of the mower drowned out the rest.

"What?" Mia cried.

Mr. Vasquez cut the motor. "I've got to mow the lawn. You girls need to play somewhere else for now." He looked around. "Where's Gabby?"

The girls all spoke at once.

"In the bathroom."

"Hiding."

"Upstairs."

"She's hiding in the bathroom upstairs,"

Mia said quickly. "We're, er, playing hide-and-seek."

"You'll have to finish your game inside. At least until I'm done out here." Her father reached down and started the mower again.

The girls trudged inside. They watched from the kitchen window as Mia's father pushed the mower back and forth. "At this rate, we'll never get back to Never Land," Kate complained.

On the windowsill, Rosetta was worried. "Isn't there some way we can stop it?" she asked Mia.

Mia shook her head. "Once he starts mowing the lawn, he always finishes. Except . . ."

"Except what?" asked Lainey.

"Well, I was just thinking of one time

when I left a jump rope on the lawn," Mia explained. "Papi didn't see it and mowed right over it. The mower jammed. He had to spend the rest of the day fixing it."

"That's what we can do!" Kate said. "We'll jam the mower!"

"No," Mia said firmly. "That's too dangerous. Papi said so. He was really mad last time. But maybe there's another way we can stop it."

Lainey was leaning out the window and studying the mower. "What's that bag on the back for?" she asked.

"It catches all the grass clippings," Mia said.

"That's what I thought," Lainey said. "Well, what if there was a little hole in

the bag. He'd have to stop and fix that, right?"

"So you're saying *we* should put a hole in the bag?" Mia thought about it. "It's not a bad idea."

"Don't you think he'd see us doing something like that?" Kate asked.

"He'd see us," Mia said. "But he wouldn't see Rosetta." The girls all turned to the fairy.

Rosetta's eyes widened. "Oh no, not me! I'm a garden fairy. Holes aren't one of my talents, remember?"

"Please, Rosetta!" Mia said. "We have to get Gabby back. Otherwise, who knows what will happen—the passage to Never Land might stay closed forever! You might never get home."

Rosetta looked from Mia to Lainey to Kate. "To think I went through all this trouble for a pretty dress. Okay, I'll do it," she said with a sigh.

The girls decided that Mia should distract her father while Rosetta made the hole. Mia found a pair of nail scissors in a bathroom drawer. They were small enough for the tiny fairy to carry.

"Be careful," Mia said as she held them out to Rosetta.

Rosetta said nothing, but she took the scissors. Clutching them against her chest, she flew out the kitchen window into the backyard.

After Rosetta was in place, Mia went out the back door. "Papi!" she shouted.

When her father turned to her, she held up a glass of lemonade. "I thought

you might need something to drink."

Her father cut the motor. "Well, that's very nice of you, Mia," he said, taking the glass. Over his shoulder, Mia could see Kate and Lainey watching. But where was Rosetta?

Then Mia spotted her. The fairy was perched on a tulip at the edge of the flower bed.

Why doesn't she go? Mia wondered. Then she noticed the flower trembling. She realized— Rosetta was scared!

Go, Rosetta, go! Mia silently urged.

After what seemed like an eternity, Rosetta lifted off the flower. She began to fly slowly toward them.

Mr. Vasquez finished the lemonade in two big gulps. He handed the glass back to Mia.

"Wait!" Mia cried, stalling for time. "Um . . . don't you want some more?"

"Not right now, thanks," her father said. "Maybe when I'm done." He reached down to start the mower.

With a jerk of the cord, the motor roared to life. Her father grabbed the handle of the mower and began to push.

Where was Rosetta? Mia couldn't see her. Had she made the hole? She glanced at the kitchen window. Kate's mouth was a round O. Lainey had her hands over her eyes.

Just then, Mia saw Rosetta. She was clinging to the mower bag as if for dear life. Then Mia's father turned the mower,

and Rosetta disappeared from view.

Mia gasped.

Suddenly, a plume of grass clippings shot from the bag like a stream of smoke. Rosetta flew around the side of the mower. She smiled and waved at Mia.

Mia's heart gave a leap. She'd done it!

"What the—" Mia's father stopped the mower. He bent to examine the bag. Then, grumbling and shaking his head, he rolled the lawn mower back toward the garage.

Now was their chance! Rosetta flew over to Mia, and Kate and Lainey hurried outside. The girls met by the fence board.

"Way to go, Rosetta!" Mia said.

"That was cool," Kate agreed. She picked up the hammer, knelt down, and began to pry at the nail.

"Hurry, Kate!" Mia crossed her fingers. "If we get Gabby back before Mami comes home, I swear I'll never fight with her again."

"I've . . . almost . . . got it!" Kate pulled

the nail free, and the board swung sideways.

"Gabby!" Mia cried, leaning through the fence. "Gabby, we're here—"

Mia broke off. Pixie Hollow wasn't there. Once again, Mia found herself staring at Mrs. Peavy's backyard. She knew they'd found the right board this time. But the way back to Never Land was gone!

Chapter 8

Iridessa scanned the trees, searching for a landmark—a twisted branch, an oddly shaped leaf, *anything* familiar. But in the growing gloom, one tree looked the same as the next.

Iridessa was furious with herself. How could she have gotten lost? And how could she have come into the forest so unprepared—without food or her basket of sunbeams or even a daisy umbrella to

stay dry? It was unlike her to do anything without a plan.

It's because of Gabby, Iridessa thought. *I let myself get distracted.* Oh, if only she hadn't agreed to look after her!

But there was nothing she could do about it now. She had to get them both out of the forest.

She fanned her wings and was relieved to discover that they had dried. She fluttered off Gabby's shoulder, where she'd been riding. "Let's hurry," Iridessa urged. "The way back must be somewhere around here."

Gabby didn't seem to hear her. She stopped to pick another dandelion.

"Come along now, Gabby," Iridessa tried again. "We haven't got time to waste.

It will be getting dark soon."

Despite the thick clouds, Iridessa could tell that the sun was lower in the sky. The day was passing quickly, and she did not want to spend the night in the forest.

Gabby blew all the seeds off the dandelion, then threw the stem away. "I'm hungry," she said.

"We'll get something good to eat just as soon as we get back to Pixie Hollow," Iridessa promised. "Acorn soup or butter cookies—anything you want!"

"I want something now." A whine crept into Gabby's voice. To Iridessa's dismay, she suddenly sat down.

"We can't stop!" Iridessa wailed. But the girl refused to budge.

Desperately, Iridessa looked around.

Her eyes lit on a bush a short distance away. It was dotted with tiny fruit. *Blueberries!*

Relieved, Iridessa flew over and plucked two berries from the bush. She handed one to Gabby. Then she settled onto a tuffet of moss to eat the other one.

As Iridessa bit into the berry, sweet juice filled her mouth. She closed her eyes. *Mmm, that's good!* She hadn't realized how hungry she was. Quickly, she gobbled up the rest.

Iridessa patted her full stomach. Then she caught Gabby's eye. The girl was watching her longingly. It would take more than a single blueberry to fill up a hungry Clumsy, Iridessa realized.

She led Gabby to the berry bush and hovered anxiously as Gabby ate her fill.

Just as Gabby finished, there was another clap of thunder. The rain began to fall again.

This time they found shelter in a mossy hollow log. As they huddled together, Iridessa stared out at the rain. She was tired, cold, dirty, and damp. She didn't know what to do. The other fairies were all so busy, Iridessa knew it would be at least another day before anyone thought to look for them.

"Tell me a story, Iridessa," Gabby said, looking out at the rain.

"We haven't got time for—" Iridessa broke off. Right now, time was all they had. They couldn't go anywhere until the rain stopped. She searched her brain for a story but found only worries. "I can't

think of one. Why don't you tell me a story instead?"

"All right." Gabby thought for a moment. "Once upon a time, there was a fairy who lived in a place called Pixie Hollow."

"What was the fairy's name?" asked Iridessa.

"Iridessa," Gabby said without any hesitation.

Iridessa smiled. "That's a good name."

"Iridessa was friends with a girl," Gabby went on. "They were very best friends. They did all sorts of stuff together."

"What kinds of stuff?" Iridessa asked.

"Like once when they went into the woods. At first the girl was a little bit scared because it was dark, but then Iridessa showed her firefly magic. And when they got hungry, Iridessa made a blueberry bush grow."

"I didn't—" Iridessa stopped. It was just a story, after all. "Then what happened?"

Gabby yawned. "Um . . . then they

went home and had hot chocolate," she murmured. Her eyelids were growing heavy. "The end."

The rain drummed on the hollow log above them. Iridessa felt herself getting sleepy, too. She brightened her glow to try to stay awake. "Everything will be okay, Gabby," she said. "We'll get home soon."

"I know," Gabby said as her eyes closed. "Because you have fairy magic." A moment later, she was asleep.

Iridessa sat watching her. She had never known anyone, fairy or Clumsy, who had so much faith in fairy magic. Gabby thought Iridessa could do anything.

If only it were true, Iridessa thought. *If only I had the right magic to help us now.*

Chapter 9

Warm sunlight touched Iridessa's face. She opened her eyes. She was lying at the entrance to the hollow log. Outside, the rain had stopped. Rays of morning sunlight shone down through the trees, making the wet forest sparkle.

Iridessa sat up quickly. She remembered that they were lost. *How could I have fallen asleep?* She turned to wake Gabby. But the log was empty.

Iridessa flew outside. She spotted the

little girl a short distance away. Gabby was staring at something in the trees.

She smiled as Iridessa flew up to her. "Look," she said, pointing.

A trail of dandelions led through the forest. All Gabby's wishes hadn't been for nothing after all, Iridessa realized. They had left a path of seeds behind them—and after the rain, the flowers had sprouted. Their yellow dandelion heads pointed the way home. There must have been some magic in those wishes for the flowers to sprout so quickly, Iridessa thought.

"Oh, you clever girl!" Iridessa cried. *All this time I thought I was taking care of Gabby,* she mused. *But really, she's been taking care of me.*

"If we hurry, we'll be back in time for breakfast," Iridessa said. "Come on, Gabby. I'll race you!"

Iridessa and Gabby arrived back in Pixie Hollow to find everything ready for a party. Colorful paper lanterns hung from the branches of the Home Tree. Walnuts roasted on spits over tiny fires, and vats of honeysuckle punch stood around the courtyard. The sound of musicians tuning their finger harps drifted through the air.

Iridessa's first thought was that Pixie Hollow was holding a party to welcome them home. Then she realized—the fairies must have finished fixing the bridge during the night. The party was to celebrate the bridge's reopening.

"Ah, home!" Iridessa exclaimed. The smell of the walnuts made her mouth water. "Come on. Let's get something to eat."

Gabby didn't reply. She looked around with a forlorn expression. Suddenly, a tear rolled down her cheek.

"What's wrong?" Iridessa asked in surprise.

"My wish didn't come true," Gabby said, then burst into tears.

Iridessa had been so happy to be back that she'd forgotten about Gabby's problem. Now she remembered how far the girl was from her own home. "Did you wish the hole would be fixed?" she asked gently.

"No." Gabby sniffled. "I wished Mia wouldn't be mad at me anymore. I wished she would be right here in Pixie Hollow waiting for me. But she didn't come. She doesn't care about me."

"Oh, Gabby, of course she does," Iridessa said.

Gabby shook her head. "She says I mess everything up."

"You don't mess everything up," Iridessa said. "You're the one who got us back to Pixie Hollow. And you rescued me from the flood. And you're the one who found all the fireflies in the forest. You did everything right. You are sweet and brave and imaginative. I would be glad if you were my sister."

Iridessa realized that it was true. If it weren't for Gabby, she never would have seen the dancing fireflies or the trail of wishes. Those things hadn't been part of her plan, but Iridessa wouldn't have wanted to miss them for the world.

Gabby had her own kind of magic, she thought. And in its way, it was as powerful as any fairy magic.

But Iridessa's words didn't seem to comfort Gabby. The tears continued to trickle down her face.

Nearby, a silver dandelion was growing in the grass. Gabby halfheartedly plucked it and blew away its seeds. "I want to go home," she said.

＊

On the other side of the fence, Mia clutched her head. "It didn't work!" she cried. "Why didn't it work?"

"Let me try," Kate said. She swung the board shut, then pulled it open again. But all they saw was the neighbor's yard.

"So I can't ever get home again." Rosetta slumped. In the wrinkled doll's dress, she looked like a wilted flower. Mia felt terrible. Just a few hours before, it had seemed like so much fun to have

a fairy living in her dollhouse. But now that it was about to come true, it felt like a tragedy.

Tears pricked Mia's eyes. "I'm so sorry, Rosetta. It's all my fault. I never should have brought you here. I should have been watching Gabby."

Mia thought of Gabby that morning. How she'd wanted to play a game. *If only I'd played with her!* Mia thought. Now she might never have the chance to play with her sister again.

Mia wasn't worried about getting in trouble with her parents. She wasn't thinking of how she'd tell Gabby off. She just wanted her sister back.

Through the screen of her tears, Mia saw something white drifting through the air. *Snowflakes—in summertime?* Mia

wiped her eyes. But then she saw that they weren't snowflakes after all. They were dandelion seeds.

Lainey and Kate noticed them, too. "Where did those come from?" Kate wondered.

Rosetta caught one of the silky seeds. She pressed it to her ear, and her eyes widened. "This seed is from Never Land!"

Mia leaped to her feet. "Are you sure? How do you know?"

Rosetta lifted her chin. "I told you, I can hear the secrets inside a seed. It's what garden fairies do."

More dandelion seeds drifted down through the air. Mia looked up and saw that they were coming from Gabby's open bedroom window.

The girls all looked at each other.

"Do you think . . . ?" Kate began.

"That the hole moved?" Lainey nodded. "It's possible."

"Anything is possible in Never Land," Mia agreed.

The girls raced into the house, with Rosetta flying behind. Mia took the stairs two at a time. When she opened the door to Gabby's room, she saw dandelion seeds drifting from beneath the closet door.

Mia held her breath, hardly daring to hope. She put her hand on the doorknob.

When she pulled the door open, she felt a warm breeze against her face. She smelled orange blossoms and sun-warmed moss.

Mia stepped through the door, crying, "Gabby! We're coming!"

chapter 10

As Mia went through the dark closet, she had a moment of doubt. What if the opening had moved on the Never Land side, too? What if it led to a pirate's ship or a dragon's lair rather than Pixie Hollow?

But a second later, Mia and her friends emerged into sunlight. They were standing on the bank of Havendish Stream. From across the stream, they could hear the lively sound of fairy music.

"I'm home! Oh, it's so good to be back!"

Rosetta exclaimed. She did a joyous twirl in the air, then darted away without a backward glance.

She didn't even say good-bye, thought Mia. But she didn't have time to dwell on that. For just ahead, standing in the Home Tree courtyard, was her sister.

"Gabby!" Mia splashed through the stream, not caring that her feet got wet. A moment later, she had her wrapped in a hug so tight that she lifted Gabby right off the ground.

"You came!" Gabby exclaimed, hugging her sister back.

"Of course I came!" Mia said. "We've been trying to get here all day."

"So you're not mad at me?" Gabby asked as Mia set her down.

"Mad? I'm furious with you!" Mia

exclaimed, giving her sister another big hug. This time Kate and Lainey joined in.

"I thought you closed the hole because you were mad at me," Gabby said.

"What? No!" Mia laughed. "We couldn't get here because Papi fixed the fence."

"And when we got the board loose again, the hole was gone!" Lainey explained.

"But you'll never believe where it showed up!" Kate jumped in. "*Your* room, Gabby! You're so lucky. You can go to Never Land anytime you want, day or night."

"No she can't!" Mia said quickly. "You're not allowed to go to Never Land without me."

"Or me," said Kate.

"Or me," added Lainey. "But I still don't understand why the hole moved."

"Never Land must want you here," Iridessa suddenly spoke up.

All the girls turned to the fairy, who was hovering next to Gabby. "What do you mean? Never Land is just an island," Kate pointed out. "How can it want something?"

"It's an island with a mind of its own," Iridessa said. "Have you ever heard the expression 'When one knothole closes, another one opens'?"

"It's 'when one *door* closes, another one opens,'" Lainey said.

"Door. Knothole." Iridessa shrugged. "Never Land must have opened a path for

you to reach it. It's the only explanation I can think of."

Mia noticed how Iridessa hovered near Gabby's shoulder. She didn't seem to want to leave her side. Mia was about to ask what Never Land wanted them for, but at that moment, Rosetta came flying back. Tinker Bell was with her.

"I told Tink all about the grass machine and the hole I put in it," she said. "She thinks she can fix it."

Tinker Bell looked excited. "It sounds like an interesting case."

"It didn't seem right to leave it for your father to fix," Rosetta explained.

"Are you sure it's a good idea to come back with us?" Mia asked. "What if the hole closes again, and you get stuck like Rosetta did?"

Tink puffed her chest out bravely. "I've been to the mainland before. I can manage."

"But you must stay for the bridge-opening party!" Rosetta clapped her hands. "A party at last! I wonder what I

should wear?" She looked down at the doll's dress, which was looking bedraggled after her adventure on the mainland. "It's a shame about this one, after all that trouble."

"We can't stay for the party. What about your mom?" Lainey reminded Mia.

"Oh! That's right. Mami is coming home any minute. We have to get back right away!" Mia grabbed Gabby's hand.

Gabby dug in her heels. "No, I want to stay."

"Gabby . . . ," Mia warned. And just like that, the two began arguing again.

At last, Mia convinced Gabby to go home, swearing that they would return to Pixie Hollow as soon as they could. They said their good-byes to Rosetta and Iridessa. Then, with Tink flying alongside

them, the girls headed back to the hollow tree.

Before she ducked inside, Mia turned for one last look at Pixie Hollow. She took in the flowers, the music, and the beautiful Home Tree, trying to tuck it all away in her memory. Mia was sure that they would be back—almost sure, anyway. But she wanted to remember everything, just in case.

Then Mia turned toward the hole that led back home. As she stepped through, she took Gabby's hand tightly in her own.

This is the end of

a

dandelion

wish

Flip the book over to read

from the

mist